At five-foot-two and skinny to boot, Maximus Bonner has always been a little sensitive about his size. When he's forced by his job to attend a team-building activity at *Rolling Meadows Ranch and Resort*, his worst fears are realized — outdoor activities. On top of that, he overhears the hottest cowboy at the place making fun of *the little stringbean*. His anger getting the best of him, Max lodges a complaint against the sexy man.

As a vampire, Rhyme Mythstone has been waiting for his beloved for over a century. Imagine his surprise when he comes in the form of a tiny slip of a redhead with a fiery temper. With one teasing comment, his chance at wooing the human goes up in flames. Max wants nothing to do with him. Can Rhyme figure out a way to prove that he loves his beloved's size and can make him happy?

Vying for his Affection
Copyright © 2019 Charlie Richards
ISBN: 978-1-4874-2668-2
Cover art by Angela Waters

Published by eXtasy Books Inc or
Devine Destinies, an imprint of eXtasy Books Inc

Look for us online at:
www.eXtasybooks.com or www.devinedestinies.com

Vying for his Affection
A Loving Nip Book 19

By

Charlie Richards

DEDICATION

Small doesn't mean insignificant. Small can be mighty.
~Unknown

CHAPTER ONE

Maximus Bonner stared out the window as he rubbed his hand over his chin. Feeling the slight rasp of his whiskers, he scratched idly. He wondered if there was a way to get out of this that he'd missed.

Probably not.

"Hey, come on. It won't be that bad." Lilibeth Shaunders tapped Max's arm where it laid on the armrest of the SUV's centrally located captain's chair, drawing his attention. "Fresh air. Hot tubs. All you can eat buffets." She waggled her eyebrows. "Hot cowboys to ogle. It'll be fun!"

Max arched his left brow. "Really? Fun?" He pointed out the window at the rolling hills, grassy meadows, and scrubby oaks. "That's nature out there. Bugs, spiders, snakes, mosquitos, and animal hair all over my clothes. That's not fun." Waving his hand at his slender body covered in charcoal gray dress slacks and a form-fitting green polo shirt, Max added, "And do you really think the cowboys are going to miss all this fabulousness?" He met Lilibeth's gaze once more, displeased to see the amusement in her expression. Huffing a sigh, Max stated, "Hello. I'm gay. I'm gonna have my ass handed to me."

"No, you won't," Lilibeth countered.

"We got your back, man," Stanton grumbled in his deep rough voice from where he sat in the middle of the rear bench seat. Due to the man's huge six-foot-five size, he had the seat all to himself. Stanton leaned forward and patted Max on the shoulder. "No one'll hurt your skinny ass while we're around.

Right, guys?"

Jerome, who was driving, simply lifted one hand from the wheel and offered a thumbs-up, obviously too busy checking the GPS and road signs. Turning in the passenger seat, George met Max's gaze and winked. "You're safe with us, Maxie."

Rolling his eyes, Max gritted his teeth at the stupid nickname that made him think of feminine hygiene products. "You know I hate it when you call me that." Max also knew that was exactly why George did it.

Asshole.

George didn't care that he was gay, at least. He just had a mouth on him. The guy was abrasive to almost everyone . . . except the bosses—Vernon and Lloyde.

The brothers owned and operated the local franchise branch of Winnerman Construction. Stanton worked as a bricklayer and made some impressive creations, while Jerome and George handled framing and drywall. Lilibeth took care of human resources. She was the one who'd put in a good word for Max when the bosses needed to hire a new accountant.

"Problem is, you all won't be around all the time," Max pointed out. "And the SUV the bosses are driving is full of homophobes and assholes."

Still, Max appreciated he hadn't needed to ride with them. He had never tried to hide his sexuality, and while the bosses didn't care, construction seemed to draw a lot of testosterone-filled jerks. The three guys and one woman in the other vehicle—Anthony, Benjamin, Curtis, and Esmerelda—took issue to the fact that Max was gay. They often made snide comments, pushed him aggressively, and smacked his shoulder or head whenever they could get away with it.

Over the three months of working at Winnerman Construction, Max had become damn good at avoiding them or making certain someone else was in the room when he couldn't.

Lilibeth's laughter filled the vehicle.

"What?" Max asked warily as he eyed his grinning friend.

Smirking, Lilibeth leaned toward him. "When I heard where we were doing this team-building activity thing, I did some research. *Rolling Meadows Ranch and Resort* is owned and operated by a pair of men . . . who are married" — continuing to grin broadly, she winked — "to each other."

"The place is run by fags?" Stanton questioned. "Oh. Sorry." He leaned forward and patted Max on the shoulder again. "Didn't mean it like that."

Max glanced behind him and offered Stanton a smile and nod, barely resisting the urge to rub his shoulder. The friendly bruiser sitting behind him really had no inkling of his own strength. He was also a kind man. There wasn't a mean bone in his body. Stanton just didn't understand that calling a gay man a fag wasn't polite.

Sadly, Stanton sort of lived up to his image — a big, dumb, gentle giant.

I like him, though.

"Well that's a relief," Max commented before humming as a smile curved his lips. "Maybe a few of the cowboys are, too. Maybe — "

He fell quiet, but Lilibeth — best friend since fifth grade that she was — must have read his mind. "Maybe a roll in the hay will be on the docket for your weekend?" she finished his sentence in a teasing tone.

Max felt his fair cheeks heat, betraying that he blushed. He hated his fair skin, but it wasn't as if he could change it. With his red hair and freckles, his skin always gave away his thoughts.

"Why would you want to roll in the hay?" Stanton asked, breaking the silence. "Didn't you just say you didn't like bugs? I figure there would be plenty in there."

To Max's relief, Lilibeth turned in her seat to answer. She

smiled widely at Stanton as she reached back and patted Stanton's knee. "If someone goes for a roll in the hay with someone else, it means they're having sex," Lilibeth explained in a blunt fashion that she only used with Stanton. At first, it had shocked Max, but now he understood it. The man needed straightforward answers.

Out of the corner of his eye, Max watched Stanton shift in his seat. He rubbed the back of his neck as a faint glow lit up his bronzed cheeks. Then he shook his head.

"Naw, Lilibeth. That can't be right. Getting naked in hay would be uncomfortable."

Jerome chuckled from ahead of them. "She's telling the truth, buddy," he countered. "Normally you lay on your clothes or bring a blanket."

"Oh. Huh." Stanton nodded as he fell silent, his gaze straying to the window.

Max had no idea how long Stanton and Jerome had been friends, but the big blond always took the wiry black man's word as gold. The pair drove in together and left together. According to the addresses for their paychecks, they lived together, but Max's gaydar said they weren't a couple.

"Slow the fuck down, Jerome," George ordered gruffly. "Or you're gonna miss the turn."

"Relax, G," Jerome replied. "I ain't gonna miss it."

Jerome did slow down, however. A few seconds later, he turned the SUV onto a gravel driveway that disappeared around a bend. Max returned his attention to the window, feeling a little better about the upcoming weekend.

If I'm going to be forced to go on this stupid retreat, at least I won't get knocked around for checking out the cowboys.

At the last monthly safety meeting—*I don't know why I have to sit in on those meetings either, but whatever*—the bosses had explained that the mandate had been passed down by the corporate office. All employees had to participate. The only reason someone could get out of it was if they'd had a doctor's note.

Oh well. At least I'm being paid for the weekend.

After the vehicle rounded the hill, Max peered out the window. "Oh, wow," he couldn't help but mutter. The place that sprawled out before them was huge.

"Aww, look at the baby cows," Lilibeth cried, pointing out the window.

"There's baby horses on this side," Max told her.

Lilibeth gasped and leaned half over him, her dark ponytail hitting him in the face.

Snickering, Max pushed her hair over her shoulder. He grinned upon seeing her smile. His old friend really did love baby animals. The only reason Lilibeth didn't have a pet of her own was because she lived in an apartment complex that didn't allow them.

"We're here," Jerome stated needlessly after he'd parked in front of a building marked *Office.*

"Good." Stanton unbuckled his belt. "I need to stretch my legs."

Jerome laughed as he opened his door, his white teeth flashing in his dark face. "It was only an hour drive," he teased before exiting the car.

As Max followed suit, he heard Stanton following as he stated, "So. I hate sitting that long."

Max glanced at the huge man, having to look up . . . and up, seeing as he only stood five-foot-two. He barely reached Stanton's sternum. "I don't like long drives, either," he commented as he took his bag from George where the other man was pulling their luggage from the back. "That's why I ride a bike to work."

"And because you can hardly reach the gas pedal of most cars," a snide voice commented with a snort. Then an elbow jabbed into Max's kidney. "Ain't that right, Max?"

"No," Max replied, stepping away from Benjamin.

Asshole.

"Lay off, Ben," Stanton ordered, using his big body to urge Max out of the way, so he could grab his own bag.

Max noticed Benjamin open his mouth, but then Lloyde rounded the back of the second SUV, and he snapped it shut again. His eyes narrowed even as he grinned at the boss. "Thanks, Lloyde," Benjamin offered as he took his bag from him.

"Head toward the office," Lloyde stated, making a shooing motion with his now-free hand. "We need to get settled in. The dinner buffet opens in thirty minutes, and I'm ready for some fried chicken."

Following everyone, Max stuck close to Lilibeth and Stanton. The woman behind the counter smiled as she greeted them—Nancy, according to her nametag. Vernon took the lead, telling her who they were and referencing their reservation.

"Of course," she replied, handing over a number of brochures. "I'm Nancy. Welcome to Rolling Meadows Ranch. Here we have calf roping, fishing, trail riding, and—"

Max allowed his mind to fade Nancy out as she spoke in favor of taking the brochure Lilibeth handed him and reading about everything himself. Trail riding did sound fun. He had no desire to learn how to rope a cow.

"Oh, look"—Lilibeth pointed to the bottom—"a hay wagon ride to a chuckwagon dinner."

"Chuckwagon dinner?" Max repeated quietly. "What's that?"

Nancy must have heard his question, for she replied, "The chuck wagon dinner is where the main food is cooked over an open fire. The meat choices are hamburger and chicken breast. There's sliced potatoes, onions, and carrots cooked with the meat, and there's also a veggie option. Other available sides are baked beans, coleslaw, mac and cheese, and for dessert, apple cobbler."

"Mmmm, apple cobbler," Stanton mumbled, rubbing his flat stomach.

After laughing lightly, Nancy returned her attention to Vernon. "Okay, then. Here are your cabin assignments." She pointed to a map on the counter that Max could barely make out. "These three here will comfortably accommodate three men each, and I figure the fourth smaller one is for the two ladies?"

"Maybe the girls and Max should take one of the trio cabins," Anthony cut in, a smirk curving his thin lips. His dark eyes were narrowed, malice glimmering in their depths. "Him being a fag and all."

"Ugh, no," Esmeralda snapped, crossing her arms over her chest. "I'm not bunking with him."

"Why?" Curtis snorted. "Not like you have anything he's interested in."

Nancy's eyes narrowed just a smidge as she glanced between the trio who'd spoken. If Max didn't miss his guess, she just managed to keep from saying something, and she didn't look pleased.

Huh. Guess this really is a gay-friendly place. Nice.

Fortunately, Lloyde spoke up. "Knock that shit off. All of you." He glanced around at everyone before ordering, "Stanton, George, and Max, you take this cabin." He handed a key to George. "Jerome, you're with me and my brother." Then he held a key out to Anthony. "You're with those yahoos, and Esmerelda, here's you and Lilibeth's key."

Max let out a sigh of relief. While bunking with George could end up annoying, what with his mouth and all, it wasn't the worst thing that could have happened.

As they all trooped out of the office and went their separate ways, with Jerome and Vernon moving the vehicles, Max wondered if the brothers knew more about the harassment that went on in their company than they let on.

And if they do, why don't they do something about it?

CHAPTER TWO

R hyme Mythstone pulled his hat off his head. With his other hand, he rubbed his bandana over his bald head, wiping away the sweat. Then he slapped his hat back on as he shoved the damp cloth into his back pocket.

"Hey, sorry I'm late."

Turning from where he was cinching the saddle on the horse tied to the hitching post, Rhyme eyed Murdoch. His brows lifted as he took in the small quarter horse mare the fellow vampire was leading. The mare was a good trail horse, but they didn't normally use her when she was pregnant . . . as she was now.

Plus, she was on the small side at only fourteen-hands, and right then, they didn't have any children at the ranch.

"Why are you bringing Lily here?" Rhyme asked curiously before returning his attention to saddling the horse — Jake.

"One of the guys that came with the construction company is a little stringbean," Murdoch told him with a chuckle. He tied Lily beside Jake and picked up a brush to start grooming her. "Gypsum thought the guy would be more comfortable riding something small."

Rhyme nodded absently. That made sense . . . except. "And Rupert wasn't available?" he asked, referring to an equally small gelding they had. They didn't keep a lot of small horses, since the ranch didn't often get children as guests.

"I checked him first, but he was limping. Looks like he threw a shoe. I took him to Abner to fix, but he was in the middle of handling Gypsum's stallion, so he could be a while." Murdoch shook his head as he winced. "And if the shoeing doesn't fix Rupert's limping, Abner will take him to London."

Reaching down, Rhyme grabbed the rear cinch and fixed it into place. "That's too bad," he commented absently as he next fitted the breast collar into position.

Murdoch just nodded as he headed to the tack room to grab a saddle for Lily.

Rhyme hoped the small gelding ended up okay. He knew if it was just a shoeing problem, Abner — the ranch's resident blacksmith and farrier — would have him sorted in no time. Well, after he finished with Gypsum's mount. The big black stallion was a damn pain in the ass, but due to size and breeding, brought the ranch a boatload of cash in stud fees.

Finishing with Jake, Rhyme moved on to the last and final horse in the line that was tied to the hitching rail. He glanced at his watch and realized he needed to hurry. Tacking up over a dozen horses for a trail ride by himself took far longer than if Murdoch had joined him as planned.

"We won't need him, since I brought Lily," Murdoch pointed out as he returned carrying a saddle.

"Right." Rhyme should have realized that. "I'm gonna put him in his paddock. Be right back."

Murdoch grunted in response, and Rhyme untied the extra horse and headed away.

When Rhyme returned, he grabbed the bottle of water he'd left on the ground near the tack shed. After twisting off the cap, he lifted it to his lips. As he gulped nearly half the bottle, he noticed the saddle Murdoch was placing on Lily.

Huh?

After swallowing, Rhyme lifted his brows in question. "Why are you putting one of our kid's saddles on her?" It was a larger kid's saddle, but it was still one they used for children. Then he grinned broadly. "Is the little stringbean really that small?"

"I'm not small. All you cowboys are just oversized," a melodious tenor snapped from behind him.

Spinning, Rhyme nearly swallowed his tongue as he looked at the speaker. He was definitely small, although it was easy to see that the guy was an adult male. Rhyme took in his skinny frame covered in relaxed jeans and a form-fitting polo shirt that just accentuated his leanness.

Rhyme took in the man's shock of red hair, flashing green eyes behind black-rimmed glasses, and the freckles on his pale features and felt his blood heat.

Cute as a button.

"Aww, don't be that way, little bit," Rhyme responded before he could think better of it—after all, the guy's crossed arms and scowling lips made his displeasure clear. Except, with arousal singing through his veins, Rhyme wasn't thinking with his big head. "You're such a tiny thing. You really could fit in that saddle."

Seeing the way the man's face flushed, Rhyme inhaled deeply as he eased a step closer. He desperately wanted to smell the fragrance of the blood filling the guy's cheeks and neck. As soon as the sweet iron-rich scent filled his nostrils, he barely managed to fight back a moan.

Exquisite.

Rhyme had never scented blood so enticing. His stomach clenched, and his mouth watered. Need for the man before him caused his half-hard dick to thicken so fast Rhyme nearly swayed on his feet.

Gods! Could this human be my beloved?

"Oh, little bit," Rhyme mumbled. "Let's go for a moonlight ride."

"Really? What the hell makes you think I'd go anywhere alone with you?" the man snapped, resting his hands on his hips. "First you insult me, twice, and now you think I'm gonna give you the time of day?" He snorted as he turned away from him, then sauntered toward Murdoch. "Looks like you got a little pony ready for me, handsome." He stopped before the animal and eyed it somewhat warily. "What's its name?"

Rhyme's stomach clenched for a whole new reason. He hated being dismissed . . . but he hated the upset scent rolling off the sexy man even more. The human who could very well be his beloved had thought he'd been insulting him.

Shit!

When Murdoch glanced Rhyme's way, a question flashing in his eyes, Rhyme mouthed, *Name?* His friend and fellow vampire offered an almost infinitesimal nod before turning his attention to the human.

"This is Lily," Murdoch told him, rubbing the mare's nose. "And she's not really a pony. She's just small for a quarter horse." Holding out his hand, he added, "What's your name?"

"I'm tired of people making fun of my size," the man stated, ignoring the question and petting the horse's neck. "You're a pretty girl, Lily. Are you a nice girl?"

"She is a nice girl," Murdoch assured. "And we pulled her out to make you more comfortable, not to make fun of you." He offered a reassuring smile as he added, "We do the same for all our guests." Pointing at a huge behemoth of a man, Murdoch told him, "Just like our friend over there is paired up with that gelding on the end."

Rhyme watched the human's eyes widen as he took in the size of the horse Murdoch had pointed out. Charlie was a seventeen-hand gelding who was part quarter horse and part friesian. They'd ended up with the animal when one of their bigger mares slipped through a broken fence and got into the pen with Gypsum's stallion. The resulting foal ended up big. Fortunately, he'd been born with his mother's sweet disposition.

"You all put your foot in it," a young woman stated from where she'd stopped beside Rhyme. She smirked at him as she held out her hand. "I'm Lilibeth. Which horse is mine?"

"It wasn't intentional," Rhyme muttered, feeling his cheeks warm. Good thing his dark skin hid such things. After a quick glance over Lilibeth's frame, he pointed toward the gelding next to Lily. "That's Jake. He's a nice boy."

"You did not just check me out," Lilibeth said with narrowed eyes.

Rhyme barked a laugh as he shook his head. "No, ma'am," he immediately assured her. "Just verifying leg length and body type so I can put you in a comfortable saddle."

Lilibeth nodded, her stance relaxing. "Okay." Then she headed toward the horse Rhyme had indicated.

Over the next several minutes, Rhyme and Murdoch went through the process of assigning horses and getting everyone comfortable in the saddle. When Murdoch moved toward the little guy at the end to finish the process, Rhyme gripped his upper arm, staying the action. "This one's mine," he murmured upon seeing the fellow vampire's surprise.

"You sure?" his friend muttered back. "Doesn't seem to want much to do with you."

"I'll have to fix that, then, won't I?" Rhyme didn't extrapolate. There wasn't time. "Start the usual spiel."

Murdoch nodded and headed toward the front of the group, not questioning him again. As a lower-ranking enforcer for their vampire coven, his buddy wouldn't question him. Murdoch would follow Rhyme's orders.

"I'm sorry you thought I was making fun of you," Rhyme stated after stopping next to the man on Lily. He rested his hand on his knee and squeezed lightly. "It wasn't my intention."

The human peered down at him with narrowed eyes. "How else should I have taken being called *the little string-bean*?" There was a snarl in his tenor voice. "Get your hand off me."

Rhyme grimaced as he lifted his hands in placation. "Okay. You're right. That was thoughtless of me." Scowling at his memory of their first meeting, he grumbled, "And you called me oversized, so I don't know if you have any room to talk. I'm only six-foot-two."

"With a giant frame," the man pointed out, stabbing his finger in the air at his torso. "Wide shoulders, big pecs. I bet you even have a six-pack under there. Anyway, it doesn't matter. Just adjust my stirrups and let's get on with this bull-shit company activity."

Swallowing hard, Rhyme tried to figure out what he could say to mend the rift that his overheard comment had created. *If he's my beloved, shouldn't the pull to bond be working in his favor?* He'd seen it happen with other vampires.

Doing as the man had ordered, Rhyme swiftly adjusted the length of the stirrups to a more comfortable position for him. Once he was done, he couldn't resist gripping his calf and helping him get his foot in the stirrup. He squeezed lightly along the skinny calf, rubbing his thumb over the faint muscle.

"Damn, you're skinny." The words were out of Rhyme's mouth before he could stop them. All his focus was on touching the slender man on the horse before him and how it made his blood burn and thud through his veins. "So fucking—"

"Shut the fuck up," the human snarled, jerking his foot away from Rhyme's hand. "I said get your hands off me."

In the process, the man slammed his heel into Lily's side. The mare jerked and shifted sideways, instantly responding to the unexpected pressure. She didn't have far to go, considering Jake stood next to her.

Still, it was enough.

The man lost his balance and tumbled toward Rhyme, squeaking in alarm. On instinct, he caught the human. As luck would have it, the man knocked Rhyme's hat from his head with his flailing limbs, then slammed one palm into his face and the other to his shoulder.

Rhyme couldn't help but gasp, which caused his fang to scrape over the human's palm. The man's blood oozed from the scratch, filling his mouth. The sweet metallic taste caused Rhyme's vampiric instincts to flare to life as his entire body surged with hunger.

Mine!

"Let go of me, goddammit!"

Coming back to himself with a mental thud, Rhyme realized that he was holding his sweet beloved around his waist. He had his face tucked against the man's neck, and he was inhaling his scent. Rhyme even rubbed his right hand up and down his near leg, since the other one was still draped over the saddle.

Lily had calmed. Probably thanks to Murdoch, who stood at her head, rubbing her nose. His fellow vampire stared at him quizzically.

Unable to explain right then, Rhyme settled his beloved, the human he hoped to soon make his forever bonded love, back into the saddle. It took every damn scrap of self-control he had to release him.

As Rhyme nodded at Murdoch and joined him before the group, he prayed his aching erection wasn't noticeable, since his flannel over-shirt was untucked. As he listened to his fellow vampire start the instruction spiel they gave every time they took a group on a trail ride, one thought reverberated through his mind.

I met my beloved, and I don't even know his name.

CHAPTER THREE

"I can't believe you filed a report on that cowboy," Lilibeth hissed as she fell into step next to Max. "Why did you do that? He was hitting on you! And he's *hawt*!"

Max rubbed the back of his neck as he winced. "Probably not my finest moment, but he just made me so mad," he admitted, glancing her way and taking in her wide eyes and parted lips. *Yep. Shocked.* "The first words I hear out of his mouth is how I'm a little stringbean. Then he calls me little bit and won't stop."

"That's because you refused to tell him your name," Lilibeth interjected.

Rolling his eyes, Max shrugged. "Well, so." *Yeah, I can be a stubborn bastard sometimes.* It came with his Scottish heritage. "Maybe he should have gotten the point and left me alone."

"Oh, come on," Lilibeth said, obviously unwilling to let the matter go. "If he'd been hitting on me, I woulda let him in my panties."

Max smirked at Lilibeth. "That's because you're a hussy."

"And you're a queen," she countered.

"And proud of it," Max responded, sticking his nose in the air.

Lilibeth laughed, then sobered. "Still . . . I'm not sure what you did was the right course of action."

Sighing, Max nodded. "I know."

"Does that mean you're gonna apologize?"

Max rubbed his hand over his face, feeling it heat beneath his palm. "I'll think about it." By then they'd reached the cabin Lilibeth was sharing with Esmerelda, and he paused at the bottom of the steps to the small porch. "How is it staying with Esme?"

It was Lilibeth's turn to shrug. "We don't really talk, so it's okay. We just stay out of each other's way." Then she started up the steps while calling over her shoulder, "See you in half an hour for lunch."

With a wave and a nod, Max started toward his own cabin. The first night hadn't been bad at all. The bedroom had two full-size beds, and the sofa had pulled out to a king size. When Stanton had asked who was going to sleep where, George had replied with, "I'll take the sofa. That way I can jack off without someone else in the room."

Yeah. That was an image Max hadn't needed to think about, but whatever. It gave him access to the bed, though, so it was cool.

Max rounded the side of the cabin being used by the bosses and Jerome, cutting down an alley. Moving quickly, he anticipated washing off the horse hair and sweat left over from the trail ride. His clothes stuck to him in places he wasn't used to, and he picked at his polo shirt, tugging it away from his chest.

"Ugh," he grumbled, when as soon as he released the fabric, it returned to clinging damply to him.

As Max walked, he thought about Lilibeth's comments. In truth, he'd been flattered by Rhyme's attention. After all, the cowboy was sexy as fuck. His broad shoulders and sculped chest beneath his open flannel and t-shirt called for Max's fingers to massage and tease. He'd so badly wanted to rub his hands over Rhyme's bald dark head.

Is he naturally smooth, or does he have slight prickles betraying he shaves his head?

If only the guy hadn't kept calling him names.

I mean, really? What the hell was that all about?

Even through it all, Max had been hard as nails. Too bad

his comments kept making Max see red. Even with his erection urging him to give in to his attraction, all Max could think
about was shutting him up.

Lost in his thoughts, Max didn't notice he had company
until someone grabbed his arm. He was jerked around to face
whoever and found himself looking up into Anthony's angry
visage. Benjamin and Curtis flanked him, their arms crossed
over their chests. All three men sneered down at him for an
instant before Anthony's shove back toward the alley caused
Max to lose sight of them.

Max's shoulder slammed into a cabin wall, drawing a hiss
of pain from him. He quickly turned so he could face his at-
tackers. Rubbing his shoulder, Max glanced between the three
homophobes he was normally good at avoiding.

Just great.

"You make me sick," Anthony snarled, stalking closer. He
cracked his knuckles as he approached. "You and the rest of
the fags around here." Glancing left and right, exchanging
nasty looks with his friends, Anthony smiled cruelly. "We're
gonna teach that cowboy fag a lesson, and you're gonna help
us."

Shaking his head, Max replied, "Why would I do that?"

"Because if you don't" — it was Benjamin's turn to crack his
knuckles and chuckle, reminding Max of a bad *Bond* villain —
"we're gonna mess you up." Then he lifted his arms and
flexed his biceps, showing off his impressive guns. "And
these babies can do some damage to a little twink like you."

Max took in Benjamin's guns, feeling impressed despite
himself. If the dark-haired man didn't have such a mean personality, he might have thought him handsome. The analogy
beauty is only skin deep popped into his head.

It sure was true with these three.

"So, I'm supposed to do . . . what?" Max asked, thinking
quickly while covertly searching for a way out.

Unfortunately, with the three much bigger men hemming

him in, he didn't see any.

"You're gonna ask that fag cowboy to talk, then take him to a secluded spot where we'll be waiting," Curtis told him, snickering. "Then we're gonna rough him up. Teach him how a real man behaves."

Max opened his mouth, then closed it again.

Shit.

While Max had been angry about Rhyme's continued short comments, he didn't want to help these assholes hurt him.

"You know, if you wanted to get me alone, all you had to do was ask."

Looking beyond Anthony's shoulder, Max felt his heart trip in his chest. Rhyme stood ten feet away. As one, the three men turned to face him, giving Max a clear view of him. The big cowboy stood with his feet braced apart and his fists on his hips. His black eyes were narrowed as he took in the interaction.

"On this ranch, we don't discriminate, so you'd best be on your way and leave Max alone."

Rhyme's deep voice held forceful authority that caused a shiver of arousal to trickle down Max's spine. His gut tightened, and his prick twitched.

Damn! Why couldn't this guy be nice?

Benjamin barked a laugh as he nudged Anthony. "This place will do, right?"

Anthony nodded. "Yep." He peered around the area. "Ain't no one around."

Fear slithered down Max's spine, replacing his untimely arousal.

Shit. They're gonna attack him!

Max thought quickly and called out, "You guys won't get away with this." He met Rhyme's gaze and asked, "Is Murdoch still at the hitching posts? I'll get him."

"He is, little bit," Rhyme drawled, his dark eyes somehow appearing to warm, even beneath the shadow of his cowboy hat. "But I won't need his help to take out these guys if they decide to get a little rough."

"Why the fuck do you insist on calling me that?" Max couldn't resist snapping, regardless of the perilous situation they were in. "You know I hate it."

Rhyme's expression actually appeared stricken. "Really?" His dark brows furrowed under his brim. "But—"

He didn't get to finish.

Anthony stepped forward and took a swing.

Rocking back a step while twisting his body, Rhyme swung his arm. He grabbed Anthony's wrist and yanked. As Anthony stumbled forward, Rhyme slammed the palm of his other hand into his torso while releasing his wrist.

Tumbling ass over teakettle, Anthony sprawled in the grass.

Benjamin and Curtis converged on Rhyme. The cowboy smirked as he glanced between them. Lifting a hand, he crooked his fingers in a beckoning motion.

Curtis lunged while Benjamin swung.

Rhyme dropped to one heel while sweeping out with his other foot. Benjamin went down. As Rhyme popped back up, he stepped close to Curtis and popped him in the gut.

With a grunt, Curtis stumbled backward a couple of steps. By that time, Anthony had risen, and he was pulling Benjamin to his feet. All three once again prepared to face off against the cowboy . . . who hadn't even lost his hat.

Glancing between them, Rhyme chuckled. "I can do this all day, boys, but you're the ones who'll be walking away with bruises," he taunted. "Not me."

"What's going on here?" a stranger's deep voice called.

Max turned and spotted a huge man in a black cowboy hat. Gaping, he realized the guy had to stand as tall as Stanton at six-foot-five. Big and broad, his presence demanded respect.

Rhyme tipped his hat at the man. "Howdy, Gypsum. These

fellers are a little bigoted and decided we fags needed to be taught a lesson." He shrugged his broad shoulders and smiled. "I was just showin' 'em why that was a bad idea."

Wait. We fags?

"Holy shit," Max muttered, staring at the man in shock. "You're gay?"

Gypsum chuckled, his pale blue eyes warming. "Never judge a book by its cover," he teased. Then his expression hardened as he crossed his arms over his chest and focused on Anthony, Benjamin, and Curtis. "We don't cotton to discrimination around here. Who are you here with?"

"They're with the construction group," Rhyme stated when the trio who'd attacked them didn't bother responding. "Had a trail ride with 'em earlier today."

"I see." A muscle ticked in Gypsum's jaw, and he turned his attention to Max. "You, too?"

"Yes, sir. I'm with the construction group," Max replied, wrapping his arms around his torso in discomfort.

Unclipping a walkie-talkie type radio from his belt, Gypsum lifted it to his mouth. "I have a situation between cabins six and seven. I need Clarice and Boyd here asap." Then he paused and added, "It might not be a bad idea if Jaymes was notified, too."

"You got it, boss." A masculine voice came through the line. "Can I give them a heads up of what's going on?"

"Yeah. A group of bigoted bullies causing trouble. Four guys from the construction company group. Find their bosses, too."

Rhyme lifted his hand, catching Gypsum's attention. "Max didn't have a part in attacking me," he said, quickly coming to his defense. As he spoke, he crossed to him. "In fact, they had him boxed against the wall and were threatening him."

Gypsum nodded once, seeming to take Rhyme's words as gold. "Three trouble makers and one who they were bothering. Rhyme stepped in to lend a hand, and an altercation broke out."

Wrapping his arm around Max's shoulder, Rhyme crooked the forefingers of his other hand and urged him to lift his chin. "You okay, little b—uh, Max?" His brows furrowed as he added, "It really was meant as an endearment because I didn't know your name."

"How did you learn my name?" Max wondered, staring into Rhyme's deep black eyes. Then he blinked, realizing who he was being comforted by. "And shouldn't you be angry with me? I complained about you to the lady at the office."

Rhyme chuckled as he nodded. "Nancy called and told me and my boss. She's the one who told me your name." Rubbing the back of his crooked fingers along Max's jawline, he crooned, "I could never be upset with you, sweetheart. Will you sit with me at lunch?" Then he cocked his head. "And you didn't answer. Are you hurt?"

Even as Rhyme spoke, he squeezed Max's opposite shoulder.

Hissing, Max cringed away from the contact.

"Damn it." Rhyme quickly lifted his hand away. "How bad is it? What happened? Can I see?"

Max's mind reeled as he tried to come to grips with what was going on. Rhyme had stepped in to help him, even after he'd reported him. On top of that, he didn't seem to be holding a grudge . . . at all . . . and he still seemed to want to spend time with him.

Why is he being so nice about everything?

CHAPTER FOUR

R hyme scented the wary unease flowing off his beloved. He hated that his earlier behavior had put it there. Still, he couldn't change who he was, and his usual personality was to tease for information.

Too bad it hadn't worked with Max.

Just means I need to work a little bit harder.

It also meant Rhyme had asked his buddy Murdoch for advice. Running across Max being bullied had been a stroke of luck . . . sort of. His vampiric instinct had been to tear the three bastards apart, and he'd barely resisted the urge to grow his claws and slice them up when they'd attacked him.

Dumbass bigots.

"You three stay put," Gypsum ordered, bringing Rhyme's attention back to where it needed to be. "We're talking to your boss about this."

Rhyme turned his attention to the trio, who stared angrily at them.

"Who the fuck do you think you are, telling us what to do," the guy who had first taken a swing at Rhyme stated belligerently. "You can't do shit to us."

"I'm someone who can kick you off the ranch," Gypsum told him coldly. "I'm sure your bosses would really appreciate being out the money of your stay due to your stupid actions and attitude."

"Damn it, Anthony," a dark-haired man grumbled as he stalked down the aisle toward them. Rhymes recognized him as Lloyde from when he and his brother, Vernon, had called to each other on the trail ride. "What the hell are you, Curtis, and Benjamin up to?"

Then Lloyde caught sight of Max and must have noticed the way he was rubbing his shoulder. His gaze flicked back to the trio and lifted a hand. "Let me guess." Pointing, he waggled it between them. "Rumpled, dirty clothes, and Max looking a little unsettled. Are you harassing him again?"

"Again?" the man addressed as Anthony replied, scowling. "What do you mean, again? We've never done anything to Maxie-pad."

Lloyde glared, and Rhyme had to bite back a growl. This was company business, so he needed to let the boss handle it. Of course, that didn't mean that if Rhyme didn't like the way Lloyde dealt with the assholes, he wouldn't track them down for a little retribution, vampire style.

Beloveds were sacred and should never be messed with.

"Don't give me that shit," Lloyde snapped at his men. "I have several documented cases, including that cheap elbow shot Benjamin gave him before we checked into the office yesterday." His eyes narrowed as he pinned his gaze on the dark-haired man. "Yeah, I saw that. You're all going through a mandatory course on harassment when we get back. Esmerelda, too." Lloyde crossed his arms over his chest. "The way you all spoke about Maximus when we checked in was the final straw, anyway."

"What?" the third man cried, a black-haired man maybe of Hispanic descent. Curtis, by default. "That's ridiculous. We've never done anything to anyone."

Lloyde scowled. "I have enough on all four of you to fire your asses, but I haven't because other than being homophobes, you do good work." Shaking his head, he warned coldly, "Don't make me change my mind." Lloyde turned his attention to Max. "Are you okay, Max? Care to tell me what happened, and I'll add it to the file."

Before Max could reply, Rhyme bit out, "You have a file on their harassment, and you're just now doing something?" His fingers itched, and it took every ounce of self-control to keep his claws from extending from his fingers. "What the hell, man?"

Gypsum's heavy hand landed on his shoulder, squeezing tightly. The order of the vampire second was clear.

Calm down.

After casting a scowl Rhyme's way, Lloyde returned his attention to Max. "I had my suspicions, but you never complained. I do wish you'd have said something, because I never caught them in the act." He shook his head as he added, "I would walk in and see you flushed and flustered or upset, but whenever I asked, you said it was nothing." Lloyde reached out and patted Max on the shoulder—the one that hurt—causing Max to flinch. Lloyde sighed, lifting his hand away. "Sorry." He turned to Gypsum. "Is there an infirmary where we can have Max checked out, please?"

"Of course." Cocking his head, Gypsum glanced from Rhyme to Max and back again.

Rhyme took the opportunity to mouth, *beloved.*

Gypsum's blue eyes lit up, and a smile curved his lips. "As soon as Boyd and Clarice arrive, I'll have Rhyme here escort you." Then he turned and spotted the pair jogging toward them. The fellow enforcers glanced around, obviously curious, but they didn't ask questions. "Excellent." Gypsum returned his focus to the trio of assholes. "We're going to escort you three to your cabin. Please stay in there for the remainder of the day. You're welcome to resume normal activities tomorrow morning."

Benjamin gaped, clearly shocked at the orders, while Curtis nodded, although his brown eyes sparked with anger.

Anthony, on the other hand, didn't take the order too kindly. "What the fuck, man?" he demanded. "You can't keep us locked up like a criminal or something."

"I was thinking more of a time out like a two-year-old," Gypsum stated, leveling a cold, narrow-eyed stare upon him. "And you will either stay in your cabin, or you can leave the ranch. Your choice."

"But we haven't even had lunch, yet," Benjamin whined, rubbing his belly, which took that second to grumble. "And we were gonna go on the chuckwagon dinner ride tonight."

"Then you really should have thought through your actions before deciding to attack your coworker and an employee of the ranch," Rhyme pointed out with a grumble. He slung his arm around Max's waist, tugging him close as he narrowed his eyes at the trio. "I can call you a cab if you'd rather leave."

"Just keep in mind, if you take that route, I'm going to have to let you go," Lloyde commented mildly. His focus flitted over the fact that Rhyme now had a quiet Max pressed close to his side, but he didn't comment on it.

"This is bullshit," Anthony snarled, but he turned to head toward his cabin.

"Don't worry," Gypsum told him coldly. "We won't let you starve. Food will be delivered."

Then the trio walked away, followed by Gypsum, Boyd, and Clarice.

"Let's get to the infirmary." Rhyme used his hold on Max's waist to start him walking. "It's attached to the back of the check-in office."

"You don't have to go with us," Max mumbled, casting a furtive glance up at him. "I don't really need the infirmary at all. I'm fine."

"You're not fine," Lloyde countered, frowning. "I saw that flinch. Did they punch you in the shoulder or something? Plus, I'd like a picture for proof."

Max sighed. "Fine. And it happened when Anthony grabbed my arm and shoved me into the wall of the cabin."

He rubbed at his shoulder in an absent manner. "I hit the wall with it."

Lloyde heaved a sigh as he nodded. "Okay." Glancing at Rhyme again, he told him, "Back of the office, huh? We can find that. You don't need to escort us."

"I'd like to, though." Rhyme dipped his head and looked at his beloved. "If it's okay with you. Then we'll go to lunch."

Max's hesitation caused Rhyme's heart rate to spike. If his beloved refused him, he would accept it . . . but he hoped he didn't. Rhyme just wanted to spend time with the man, maybe figure out a way to communicate a bit better.

"I-I, um . . . sure. I guess?"

Not exactly a great vote of confidence, but Rhyme would take it. "Thank you, Max."

"Hey, Lloyde!" The man's brother came jogging over to them, his brows furrowing as he took in Rhyme's possessive hold. "Uh, what's going on?"

As they walked, Lloyde explained what he knew. Then Max and Rhyme filled in the missing pieces. By the time they were done, Vernon was damn near seething.

His face red with his anger, Vernon snapped, "I told you we should have fired those assholes months ago."

Rhyme bit back his grumbled response of, *then why didn't you?*

Instead, he listened as Lloyde lifted his hands in placation. "I know, Vern, but we can't change the past. They're going through a harassment seminar, and I told them if they didn't want to do that, we would be letting them go."

Max snorted. "You really think that sort of shit works?"

"Maybe not," Lloyde countered. "But no more hiding harassment shit. Got it?"

Sighing, Max admitted, "I didn't think you'd believe me." He offered his bosses a small smile. "After all, they've been there years, and I'm the new guy here."

"Yeah, but you're not the only one at the company who's gay," Vernon stated, his smile wry.

Max gaped.

"You or your brother?" Rhyme couldn't swallow the words. His curiosity just got the better of him sometimes. Both men peered at him with their eyebrows raised, so Rhyme grinned and added, "Or both of you?"

Lloyde laughed as he knocked his shoulder into Vernon. "Both of us, not that we're as out and proud as you two." His brown eyes sparkled with mischief as he glanced between them. "Are you even gonna use that bed we're paying for this evening?" he teased. "Or is George not gonna sleep on the sofa tonight?"

As Rhyme watched, Max's face turned bright red. Then his eyes narrowed, and he opened his mouth. Rhyme just bet he was about to say something scathing to his bosses.

While part of Rhyme wondered what he would say, he didn't want to put his beloved on the spot, either. To head off losing the bit of ground he'd gained in the last half hour, Rhyme answered first.

"I don't want Max to think this is just a vacation fling to me," Rhyme stated quickly. His eyes narrowed as he pinned a hungry look on his beloved. "Although I would love to take you back to my room and worship every inch of your body for hours, I'll settle for cuddling on the hayride tonight. Perhaps a walk in the moonlight after that." Tracing the fingertips of his free hand along Max's jaw, he admired the wide-eyed, shocked expression on his human's freckled face. "Maybe a goodnight kiss, too, if you'll let me?"

"Y-You're attracted to me?" Max sounded shocked.

Both bosses barked out a laugh, drawing his beloved's attention. He scowled at them. They exchanged a look as they shook their heads.

"If you hadn't been so focused on the fact that Rhyme was

calling you little bit, you would have understood the inflection," Lloyde began.

"Or noticed the obvious attraction," Vernon cut in, rolling his eyes. "Hell, it sounds like even those three idiots caught on, and they're pretty damn thick about that kind of stuff."

"Caught on?" Max glanced around at the three of them, his face turning the slight pinkish hue that Rhyme was coming to love. "What do you mean? Caught on to what?"

Lloyde smiled down at Max. "When he calls you little bit, it's a term of endearment."

Max scowled. "No way." Rhyme nodding must have caught his attention, for he stared up their foot height distance and gaped. "Really?"

"Yeah." Rhyme squeezed Max's waist as he added, "I love your size. It's perfect for snuggling you into my side." Massaging his hip a little, he added, "I'd love to map every damn one of your sexy freckles, and — "

"And we've probably heard more than we need to," Lloyde stated on a laugh. "Let's get you checked out so we can head to lunch."

Rhyme chuckled, just remembering to keep his grin contained enough to hide his fangs. The day was looking up.

CHAPTER FIVE

After the most humiliating fifteen minutes of his life, where his bosses took pictures of not only the bruising already starting on his shoulder, but of the already developed mark from where Benjamin had nailed him in the back, Max was finally on his way to the dining hall for lunch. He'd always bruised really easily. With his fair skin, he'd dealt with the issue his whole life.

At least Doctor Madilyn Dozers had made Rhyme stand in the hall. He didn't think he could handle the big cowboy's scrutiny on his body just yet. Max figured he would either pop wood—which would totally suck seeing as his bosses were there—or he would turn into a red ball of embarrassment.

Max knew from experience that his blushes went all the way down his torso. Damn his fair skin. The fact that Rhyme had mentioned his freckles only compounded the problem.

Did Rhyme really have some weird freckle fetish?

Dismissing the thought when the dining hall came into view, Max felt his stomach rumble. His mouth watered, and he swallowed twice. He couldn't wait to see what the place was serving. Their huge breakfast spread had been epic, and Max had eaten so much he hadn't thought he would need more food for the rest of the day.

He was wrong.

Huh. Must be all the physical activity—horseback riding, then hiking between buildings on the ranch.

Max smiled.

Na. I'm always hungry.

Then the rich aromas of assorted cooked meats flooded his nostrils, and he groaned softly. "Oh, god." Rubbing his belly, he quickened his pace.

"Hungry, handsome?" Rhyme asked with a smile on his wide lips. When Max nodded, the much bigger man hummed. "Me, too."

Rhyme opened the door of the dining hall and stood back as Max entered along with Lloyde and Vernon. He still reeled a bit at the revelation that both his bosses were gay. Although, that did explain why they were so accepting of Max's occasional outrageous attire and how he changed the color of his nails every few days.

Speaking of which . . .

Max glanced at his hands and winced. "I need to wash up," he murmured, seeing the dirt under his neon green nails. He turned in time to see Rhyme hanging his black cowboy hat on one of the hat-racks by the door. "Is there a men's room here, or do I need to go back to my cabin?"

"This way," Rhyme said, resting his hand on Max's lower back and urging him to the left. "I need to wash up, too."

Doing his best to keep his breathing deep and even, Max thought unsexy thoughts. The feel of Rhyme's big black hand on the small of his back just felt too delicious. It was as if the heat of it transferred straight through his body and gripped his dick in a hot hold.

Oh god! Stop thinking like that.

Those thoughts were causing his blood to flow south, and his balls began to tingle.

Shit. Okay. Okay. Skunks. My grandmother's panties. Mosquitos and ticks. My dad.

That did the trick. One thought of his father yelling about how Max was an abomination and would burn in hell and his dick tried to crawl back up into his body.

"For a second there, you were thinking of something pleasant," Rhyme rumbled into his ear, bending his body to do so as he pushed open a door with a cowboy on it. "Then that changed. Is everything okay?"

Gasping, Max peered over his shoulder as he headed inside first. "H-How did you know that?"

Rhyme's full dark lips curved into a slight smile. "Your facial expression." He touched his jaw lightly. "You're very expressive."

"Then how come you didn't know I was pissed off at you earlier today?" Max couldn't help but snap. The man had been annoying in his pushiness, even as Max had found him sexy and distracting. He knew that was why he'd reacted so intensely.

Chuckling, Rhyme made his way to a urinal. Even as he began to unbuckle his belt, then undo his fly, he peered over at Max and winked. "I was too busy getting drunk off your cologne and being blinded by your stunning features."

Max gaped. "Are you for real?"

Rhyme nodded once, then heaved a deep sigh. Tipping his head back, he closed his eyes, then took a deep breath before letting it out between pursed lips. After he did that a second time, Max cocked his head.

"Are you okay?"

Humming, Rhyme murmured without opening his eyes. "Will be. Having you close is giving me a boner, but I really gotta piss. Just give me a sec."

Once again, Max's jaw sagged open as shock filled him. Unable to help himself, he did the unthinkable and focused on Rhyme's groin. His breath caught in his throat at the beautiful brown piece of meat that jutted half-hard from the big cowboy's groan.

"Oh, god," Max whispered as his asshole clenched. He loved a big dick splitting him wide open . . . and Rhyme's was a thing of beauty and would do exactly that. His blood heated, and his cock hardened in his jeans. "R-Rhyme."

As Max watched, Rhyme's cock twitched and began to thicken even more.

Rhyme moaned as he opened his eyes. Turning his attention to Max, he stared at him with a feral hunger gleaming in his black eyes. "Baby, unless you plan to step into the handicap stall with me and do something about this, I need you to control yourself."

Max swallowed hard upon seeing the need in Rhyme's eyes. *Oh wow.* A second later, his cheeks went up in flames, and he felt the blush to his toes . . . and his cock.

Realizing he had a stiffie from just that look from Rhyme, Max tore his gaze away from the gorgeous specimen before him. "I-I'll, uh, just, um . . . yeah." Pivoting, Max strode to the sink and turned on the water. For the next minute, he focused on scrubbing the dirt off his hands and out from under his fingernails. Seeing the chipping on his polish certainly helped his dick relax. He tried to remember if he'd brought any and realized with relief that he had a bottle of pale purple with him.

Nice. I'll fix this tonight.

Then Max wondered if he had any remover. He didn't think so. Hearing the sound of piss hitting a bowl, Max remembered he wasn't alone.

"You know if anyone here has nail polish remover?" Max figured it couldn't hurt to ask. "Maybe in your gift shop or something?"

Rhyme hummed, indicating that he'd heard him. It took a few seconds before he replied, however. Finally, he offered, "I'll ask around. I bet someone here has some."

"Thanks." Max smiled at his hands, pleased to see that they were finally clean. "So much better."

Then Max splashed some water on his face before patting it dry with a paper towel.

"You're sexy when you're dripping wet," Rhyme whispered huskily from where he stood beside him, washing his hands.

Max rolled his eyes as he smirked at the man. "Really? I'm washing my face, and you're calling me sexy?"

Finding it cute, Max was beginning to realize that Rhyme really just had no filter. He said just about everything that popped into his head. The trait in the huge man was sort of . . . endearing.

Rhyme waggled his eyebrows. "Just calling it like I see it."

"Then you need these glasses even more than I do."

Barking a laugh, Rhyme shook his head as he dried his hands. Once done, he grabbed Max and pulled him into a hug. Rhyme dropped a quick kiss to Max's temple while whispering, "I'm right," before releasing him and stepping backward. "You gonna pee, or are you done?"

"You are really blunt," Max couldn't help but comment as he started toward a stall. "And, yeah, I gotta pee."

"No urinal for you, huh?" Rhyme teased as he rested his rear on the counter and crossed his arms over his chest. His smirk was firmly fixed on his face as he leveled a heated gaze on Max.

Pointing at Rhyme, Max stated, "And that right there is why I'm going into a stall."

"Aww." Rhyme curved his lips in a pout that looked absolutely ridiculous on the big man's face. Then he whined playfully, "But you saw me."

Max laughed as he stepped into the stall. "That was your choice," he called as he locked the door and undid his pants.

As Max stood over the toilet and aimed, mentally urging his bladder to relax and let it all go, he heard Rhyme's deep voice from just outside the stall. It sent a shiver of desire down his spine.

"I loved the look of appreciation in your eyes, sweet man,"

Rhyme rumbled, his tone husky. "When we come together, the feel of our bodies sliding against each other will be even better, and I plan on putting that hungry look on your face often."

Gritting his teeth, Max muttered, "R-Rhyme, pl-please." His balls tightened, and his blood began to fill his prick. "Not nice."

"Gods, the sound of you begging is so pretty," Rhyme said on a hum. To Max's relief — or disappointment, depending on how he looked at it — Rhyme next purred, "I'll be waiting right outside, Max."

Max panted harshly as he listened to Rhyme's booted feet thud across the floor, then exit the room. Blowing out a harsh breath, he once again pulled up the mental image of his father. His shaggy red hair framed his chubby red and freckled face as he yelled slurs and threats. Then Max recalled the pain of the man's backhand, and a shudder worked through him . . . and not the good kind that Rhyme caused in him.

A second later, Max heard urine hit the bowl and snapped his eyes open.

Whew! I didn't miss.

That would have been embarrassing.

Max quickly finished up, tucked himself away, and washed up. Slipping out of the room, he found Rhyme leaning against the wall, waiting, just as he said he would be. The big cowboy smiled, then his eyes narrowed.

"Is everything okay?" Rhyme asked.

Surprised at the question, Max nodded. "Yeah. Why wouldn't it be?"

Rhyme shook his head once, but the question remained in his eyes. "Just how dark the green of your eyes is, says you're upset." When Max opened his mouth to question that, Rhyme took his hand and squeezed while telling him, "Hell, I saw it often enough this morning, so now I recognize it."

Fighting the urge to grumble under his breath, especially

in lieu of Rhyme's self-depreciating smile, Max admitted, "Just had to think unsexy thoughts to get rid of the erection you gave me." Then he fought the blush erupting over his cheeks.

Great.

Rhyme's booming laugh filled the room as he guided Max back into the main area and led him toward the buffet. The noise drew everyone's attention. While most of his coworkers appeared amused, Max saw the hateful glare covering Esmerelda's features.

Wonder what's up her butt this time.

Then Max recalled Lloyde's mandate that she take the harassment course, too. He wondered if his boss had already told her. It wouldn't surprise Max that she blamed him . . . even though it was her own behavior that landed her in the course.

Allowing Rhyme to guide him toward the food — after all, his stomach was growling something fierce — Max did his best to ignore her.

CHAPTER SIX

A s Rhyme watched Max load his tray with food, and a lot of it, he wondered how the skinny human could hope to get through it all. He knew better than to ask him, however. Instead, he would watch and learn.

Rhyme loved the fact that his words had gotten his human so hot he'd had to think of unsexy things to deal with it. He'd had to do the same thing. The only problem was, it was harder to deal with his beloved's sweet scent permeating the room.

He'd had to recall the smell of a rotting cow corpse he'd come across while looking for strays. The animal had been dead for at least a week. From the looks of things, a cougar had taken it down but hadn't eaten it all. He could only guess at why, but the smell of the beast had been rancid.

Settling in a chair next to Max, who had chosen to sit at the table with the others from his company, Rhyme spotted the amused expression on Lilibeth's face. The bosses nodded at him in greeting but continued to chew their food in silence. The other men each reached out a hand and introduced themselves—Jerome, Stanton, and George. Only Esmerelda completely ignored him.

Fine by me.

Rhyme talked a little with the guys as he ate, asking them about working in construction. To his amazement, Max actually managed to eat just about everything on his plate. His beloved seemed to be a bottomless pit, and he didn't talk much, probably due to the knowing looks he was receiving from Lilibeth.

As Rhyme watched Max eat, he realized his beloved wasn't purposefully ignoring him. Instead, it almost seemed as if he were constantly keeping an eye out to see if someone would steal his food. Finding that odd, Rhyme decided to test that theory.

Since his own plate was empty, Rhyme reached out with his fork and scooped up a forkful of cheesy, hashbrown casserole. As he brought the food to his lips, he saw the way Max froze. His beloved didn't move so much as cut a wide-eyed gaze his way.

Then Max's eyes narrowed as he used his own fork to point toward the buffet. "You know, if you wanted some, there's a whole tray full up there."

Rhyme smiled at his human, doing his best to look disarming. As he spoke, he wasn't certain it worked, but now he had his answer. His beloved was overprotective of food.

Huh.

That spoke of something in his childhood.

"Sorry, beloved," Rhyme murmured, glancing over his shoulder at the bar. "Yes, there's definitely a fresh tray full." He tipped his chin toward the remaining hashbrown casserole on Max's plate. "That stuff is always a crowd-pleaser, regardless of the meal. I didn't take any and wanted a taste."

"Then why didn't you get some?" Max asked with a wary expression.

Rhyme set his fork down, then rested his hand on Max's thigh. He rubbed lightly as he told him, "I'm full."

Max frowned. "Then why did you steal my food?"

"Oh, you've done it now," Stanton commented with a low chuckle. The huge lug of a man leaned toward him, his elbows on the table. "No one steals Max's food."

Humming, Rhyme nodded his head. "I see." He winked at Stanton, saying, "Fortunately, I know just how to make it up to him."

After another quick glance at Max's plate, Rhyme rose and

headed toward the buffet. He grabbed a sugar cone from the dispenser, then, with ease that betrayed he'd used the machine a lot, he prepared a cone of twist ice cream. As he returned to the table, much to his satisfaction, he noticed the vanilla and chocolate swirls nearly lined up damn perfectly.

"Here you go," Rhyme stated, holding it out. To his pleasure, Max's green eyes lit up behind his black-rimmed glasses. When he reached for it, Rhyme resisted the urge to take a lick before handing it over. Instead, he stated, "Next time I steal your food, I'll repay it with a hot fudge sundae. How's that sound?"

Max's eyes narrowed, and he stared intently at him. After several heartbeats, he nodded once. "Okay." Then he took a long lick of the ice cream cone.

Rhyme barely managed to hold in his moan. The image of Max licking his erect dick just that same way flashed through his mind. Unable to help himself, he reached down and adjust his quickly hardening shaft.

Just damn.

Obviously realizing what he was doing to Rhyme, Max smirked and continued to eat his ice cream cone.

"God, it's like watching porn," Lilibeth commented, breaking their stare-down.

Clearing his throat, Rhyme appreciated his dark skin color, hiding the fact that his cheeks were heated. Max was not so lucky, and his pale cheeks took on an impressive pinkish hue. Lowering his gaze, his beloved focused on finishing his treat.

"Disgusting." Esmerelda jumped from her seat and stalked out of the room.

"Well that was rude," Stanton stated, frowning at where Esmerelda had been sitting. "She didn't even throw away her garbage."

"That's not the only reason she was rude." Jerome reached over and touched Stanton's tanned forearm with one of his long, slender, black-skinned fingers. It drew the huge man's gaze, who sported a confused expression. "She called the sexual attraction between Max and Rhyme disgusting."

Stanton glanced between them. While his cheeks darkened just a smidge, he cocked his head. Then he nodded.

"Yeah, she thinks guys that like other guys are gross. I've heard her talk about it sometimes." Stanton focused on Jerome. "Why would she care what people do in their bedroom? What's it to her?"

"That's the point, Stanton my man," George commented while dunking his roast beef sandwich into a cup of au jus sauce. "She shouldn't care. Ain't nobody's business what our dicks get up to but us and whoever we're with." The dark-haired man rolled his eyes as he lifted his sandwich to his lips. Before he took a big bite, George finished, "If you or me wanna bugger another guy or fuck a lady in the ass, that's between us and them, but Esmerelda's a stuck up bitch who can't get her head out of medieval times."

Stanton looked a little confused. The bosses appeared a smidge pained, as if they weren't certain if they should admonish their employee or not. Max remained focused on his ice cream, and Lilibeth was nodding.

Jerome patted Stanton's arm. "Don't try to understand someone who's so hateful, Stan. It's a waste of time."

Even as his light-brown eyebrows furrowed, Stanton nodded. "Right." Then he rose from his seat and rounded the table. "I'll take care of this."

As Rhyme watched, the man he realized was a gentle giant cleaned up after the pretty yet hostile Esmerelda.

Huh.

Rhyme found he liked the big human. He was . . . sweet. Cocking his head, he made a note to text every available vampire in the coven to make an effort to meet the man. Since Fate had been so kind to him, maybe she would be kind to one of his fellow paranormals and pair them up with this good-natured human.

Saying goodbye to Max without kissing him was tough. Rhyme desperately wanted another taste of his beloved's blood. He also wished he could spend all afternoon wooing him, but Rhyme had things to do.

Plus, Max was supposed to be there for team building with his company. Although, Rhyme wasn't certain how much of that would be accomplished since three of the employees were under house arrest for the evening.

"Can I pick you up at your cabin, Max?" Rhyme asked while squeezing his human's hand. "Say, half an hour before the dinner ride is supposed to start?"

After a second of hesitation, Max agreed.

Rhyme squeezed Max's hand one more time, then released him. Heading toward the horse pens, he had another trail ride to get ready for. At least the work would keep his mind occupied . . . mostly.

As Rhyme walked away, his sensitive vampiric hearing allowed him to catch Lilibeth's whispered comment of, "What the hell, Max? You were complaining about him when you dropped me off at my cabin. Then you're late for lunch, and he's with you. What happened?"

Grinning, Rhyme wished he could hear Max's response, but even his hearing wasn't that good as he continued to stride away from the group.

Upon reaching the paddocks, Rhyme began pulling out their trail mounts for the afternoon rides. There were three scheduled, each one lasting around an hour. Due to the summer heat, the long rides were taken in the morning.

"Hey, Rhyme," Murdoch greeted, entering the pen with a couple of halters of his own to grab a pair of horses. "I woulda thought Master Jaymes would have given you the afternoon off to spend with your beloved."

"He offered," Rhyme told his oldest friend. "But after what happened on the ride this morning, I explained I needed to slow-roll it. Ya know?" Then Rhyme chuckled as he shook his head. "I was still in the office when Nancy called and told the master that Maximus had complained about me."

Murdoch barked a laugh as they both led a pair of animals out of the corral, locking the gate behind them. "I bet he got a kick out of that." Smirking, he added, "Did you finally stop calling him little bit?"

Wincing, Rhyme nodded while tying up the pair of horses he had led to the hitching rails. There were three pipe-rails, and each had hooks spread along it so six horses could be tied to it at a time. They were at intervals so there was plenty of room to walk around each animal.

"So you're slow-rolling it, huh?" Murdoch asked as he tied up his horses nearby. "What's your plan?"

Rhyme grinned broadly at his friend. "Actually, I had lunch with him, and I'm taking the evening off to go on the chuckwagon dinner ride with him."

Upon seeing Murdoch's questioning look, Rhyme explained everything that had happened over the last hour and a half.

Murdoch grinned broadly. "Nice!"

Nodding happily, Rhyme headed back to the barn to check the list. Once he'd ascertained how many horses they would need for that afternoon's rides, he grabbed a couple more halters and returned to the paddocks.

Time flew as Rhyme worked. Chatting with guests and sharing information about the horses they rode and the land they traveled through kept his mind mostly occupied. Fortunately, that helped ease the arousal that had been thrumming through his body since that morning.

Riding with a boner sucked. He should know. He'd done it for nearly three hours just that morning.

With the final trail ride complete and the guests on their

way to other activities, Rhyme began unsaddling horses.

Murdoch tapped him on the shoulder and made a shooing gesture. "Go get cleaned up. That ride took a little longer than anticipated since that one lady was frightened to go down the hill and had to be led." He tapped his watch and added, "Don't want to be late."

"Thanks, man," Rhyme commented as he checked the time on his phone. He winced, seeing he only had a little over an hour before he'd told Max he would pick him up, and he had a few things he needed to get done first. "See you later."

Rhyme took off, jogging down the gravel road to the office where there was a small gift shop. Unfortunately, they didn't sell nail polish remover. He headed to the main house.

While a few who were bonded had chosen to build small homes of their own deeper on the property, most vampires stuck together . . . especially since Master Jaymes's ranch home was huge with plenty of spacious suites. Stopping in the main lounge, he spotted Madilyn, their coven's doctor. When he called her name, she lifted her focus from the e-reader she'd been perusing.

"Hey, Rhyme," Madilyn greeted with a smile. "I hear congratulations are in order."

Rhyme grinned as he nodded. "The grapevine is alive and well, I see."

"You know it." She winked.

"I was hoping you could give me a hand," Rhyme admitted, stopping beside the sofa.

Madilyn put her reader down. "Sure. What's up?"

Appreciating her instant agreement — hell, finding your beloved was the most important moment of any vampire's life, and most would do whatever they could to facilitate it — Rhyme explained that he was looking for nail polish remover.

"I don't think I have any, but I'll check." Madilyn rose from her seat, grabbing her reader and heading toward her suite.

As she moved, she called over her shoulder, "But I bet Doris has some if I don't. I'll find some for you."

"Thanks, Madilyn." Rhyme headed toward his own suite.

After a quick shower and shave, Rhyme pulled on his clothes. He slid his feet into his dress boots. Another glance of the time showed him he had ten minutes.

Rhyme took a couple of those to focus on deep breathing. The anticipation filling him caused his blood to heat and his nerves to sizzle. He needed to calm down, or he would be sporting an uncomfortable erection for the entire evening.

"Shoulda jerked off in the shower," Rhyme grumbled, but he'd been in a hurry.

A knock at his suite's door drew his attention, and Rhyme crossed to it. To his pleasure, he found Madilyn standing on the other side of it . . . and she was holding a bottle.

"Sweet. Thanks!" Rhyme took it and headed out to fetch his date for the evening.

CHAPTER SEVEN

"You're as nervous as a cat in a room full'a rocking chairs," Jerome commented from his seat on the sofa. He sported a smirk as he watched Max pace, sit on the sofa for a few seconds, then pop up and begin pacing again.

Max had been surprised to find that Stanton had a neat streak in him and had ordered George to put his bed away for the day. To his even greater shock, George had bobbed his head in a nod while saying, "Was gonna anyway."

While Max didn't know if that was true, at least they had a place to sit other than the desk chair. Taking a seat on the edge of the sofa again, he rubbed his palms over his thighs. "He's really attractive, and he helped me, but I—" Max paused and shook his head.

"If you like him, why are you so worried?" Stanton asked from where he sprawled on the desk chair. "Attraction is important if you're going to date someone. Even when it's two guys, right?"

Glancing between the two men, Max felt relieved that George had already left. The man had met a woman there with a couple of lady friends, and for some reason, she was attracted to George. He was on his way to escort her to the wagon.

Kinda like what Rhyme is doing for me.

"Attraction is important," Max replied slowly. "But what I feel for him is . . ." He wasn't certain how to describe it.

"Overwhelming?" Jerome offered helpfully. The black man grinned when Max met his gaze. He winked, adding,

"The only reason to get so pissed off at someone teasing you is if you're attracted to him, and you think they're making fun of you."

Groaning, Max covered his face with his hands. "Was I that obvious?"

"Not to me," Stanton told him.

Unfortunately, that didn't reassure Max much. He liked the huge bricklayer, who could design some of the most exquisite things with stone, but Stanton missed a lot of social nuances. His brain just didn't work that way.

"I still don't understand the problem." Stanton scowled as he rubbed his huge palm over his buzzed blond hair. "You like him, so you date to get to know him." Then something must have occurred to him. "Unless you just want to fuck. Is that what you want? A vacation fuck and he said you weren't doing that tonight?"

Max's body flushed hot with arousal, and his cock thickened in his jeans. Groaning, he cupped himself. Just thinking of getting fucked by the huge piece of meat that he'd seen jutting from Rhyme's groin caused his body to nearly erupt with need.

Jerome laughed, shaking his head. "God, man." He stared at Stanton and told him, "I think Max's trouble is he *wants* to be fucked by Rhyme, but he doesn't want to look easy on the first date." Then he waggled his eyebrows as he focused back on Max. "But you would *love* to be that easy, wouldn't you, Max?"

"Oh, god, yes," Max admitted on a groan, pressing the heel of his palm against the base of his prick. "I want his dick in me so fucking bad, I—" Realizing what he'd just admitted to his coworkers, men he didn't really know all that well, his face erupted in flames as he muttered, "Sorry."

Shrugging his lean shoulders, Jerome glanced pointedly at Max's fly. "Maybe you oughta jack off before he gets here.

You're a little primed there."

Max groaned as his embarrassment grew by leaps and bounds. Fortunately, that caused his erection to flag. He glared at Jerome.

Jerome just smirked.

"Doesn't taking something as big as a guy's dick up your ass hurt?" Stanton shifted in his seat, as if he felt discomfort upon only thinking about it. His eyes narrowed. "I mean, your ass is really small, and Rhyme is really big, so—"

Unable to help himself, Max felt his jaw sag open.

Even Jerome's dark eyes had widened by the time Stanton's voice trailed away.

Obviously realizing what he'd just asked, the man's cheeks darkened to a bright shade of pink. "Um."

A hard knocking sound interrupted them.

Whew!

Max bounced off his seat and crossed to the door. After a deep breath, he opened it. His breath left him in a whoosh upon seeing the handsome cowboy standing on the other side.

"Wow," Max whispered, unable to help taking in the man before him.

Rhyme's gray and brown boots appeared to be made of some kind of snakeskin. His long, muscled legs were encased in form-fitting, faded jeans. The red, pearl-snapped shirt fit his torso like a second skin, leaving nothing to the imagination.

Yep. Six-pack. Delicious!

When Max's gaze finally landed on Rhyme's face, the cowboy sported a crooked smile, and his eyes appeared to glitter in the shade of his black-brimmed cowboy hat.

"Oh, sweetheart," Rhyme rumbled, his voice thick and husky. "As much as I love the way you're looking at me right now, I'm not certain we have time for that."

"I don't know about that," Jerome drawled from behind

them. "Pull him onto your lap on the sofa, get your dicks out, and jack 'em." He snorted as he leaned a forearm on the doorframe and swept his gaze up and down them both. "I bet neither of you would even make it ten strokes."

Max gaped at Jerome.

Rhyme snorted. "You're awfully comfortable with talking about gay sex," he pointed out while holding out a small bottle to Max. "Somethin' you want to share with the class?"

Listening to Jerome chuckle as he moved past them, it took Max a second to realize what Rhyme was giving him. Upon recognizing the polish remover, he grinned widely. "Thank you so much!" he cried, taking it and placing it on the stand just inside the door.

"You're welcome, Max," Rhyme replied, looking pleased with himself. Then he winked at Max before returning his focus to Jerome and lifting a brow in question.

Jerome shrugged. "My little brother came out as gay when he was sixteen. I was twenty-two." His expression sobered as he added, "He moved in with me because my parents disowned him." Crossing his arms over his chest, Jerome glanced between them. "I ended up doing a lot of research to help him stay safe and take care of himself."

"You're a good brother," Max whispered.

Upon hearing the tale, Max thought about his own older brother. He hadn't been nearly so understanding. In fact, he'd helped their father not only kick him out of the house but drive him out of the county. It was a good thing he had Lilibeth to turn to. She'd allowed him to surf her couch until he'd found a job and got his feet under him.

"Hmm, I get the feeling something in that story reminded you of your own coming out," Rhyme commented, picking up his hand and threading their fingers together. "And your big brother didn't help."

Squeezing Rhyme's hand as he met his understanding

gaze, Max shook his hand. "No. I had Lilibeth."

Rhyme used his hold to reel him closer, releasing him so he could slide both arms around him. "I'm glad you had her." Hugging Max to his chest, he pressed a nuzzling kiss to his temple.

"Sorry to ruin the moment," Jerome murmured, shifting his weight uncomfortably.

"It wasn't you," Max assured, pulling away so he could smile at the framer who could very easily become a good friend. Then he smirked as he glanced around at the other guys. "At least now I'm not going to be uncomfortable on the hayride."

Jerome barked a laugh, his relief filling his expression. "Right." He rolled his eyes. "So glad I could help."

"Actually, me, too," Max admitted.

"I'm hungry," Stanton commented, closing the cabin door. "We going?"

"Definitely." Rhyme released his hold on Max and took his hand again. "Come on." As they walked, he dipped his head and told him, "And you look amazing, too, handsome."

"Too?" Max didn't remember complimenting Rhyme.

Rhyme waggled his brows, perhaps reading his mind. "You gave me a hell of a compliment with your expression when you opened the door."

"Oh." Max felt his cheeks heat, and he knew he blushed.

"So gorgeous, Max," Rhyme purred huskily, reaching over to trace a fingertip down his neck. "Can't wait to see more of it."

Max's shaft began to thicken anew, and he groaned. Pushing Rhyme's hand away, he grumbled, "Behave."

"For now," Rhyme agreed with a cheeky smile.

Max enjoyed the hayride, and Rhyme behaved the perfect gentleman. He helped Max into his seat, even draping one of the provided blankets over the hay bale for his comfort. With his arm around Max's shoulders, Rhyme kept him from being jostled too badly while the team of draft horses pulled the wagon.

"I've never been on a hayride where it was pulled by horses before," Lilibeth commented from where she sat on Max's other side. "It's always been pulled by a tractor."

"We do have a tractor that can pull this. We use it when we load hay bales onto this from the field," Rhyme admitted. "But we thought having it pulled by horses for the dinner would be more authentic."

"You have your own hay fields?" Lilibeth glanced around, but all around them were sparse copses of trees and rolling meadows. "Where?"

"We do," Rhyme confirmed, pointing over his shoulder with his thumb. "When you first enter the ranch, there's a gate into the left pasture. Cross that to another gate, and there's a dirt road which leads to them." Smiling, he told her, "You should come back during October. We use the hay bales to form a haunted maze out there. People park in the pasture, then take a hay wagon to the maze." Shrugging, he added, "Although that's pulled by our tractor. Unless people want to walk, anyway."

"Oh, wow! You guys do a maze?" Stanton cut in from where he sat on Rhyme's other side. "That'd be fun." Then his brows furrowed. "Or would I be too tall and could see over the side?"

Rhyme patted Stanton's knee good-naturedly. "Nope. Don't you worry about that. We make our walls seven feet high. You won't be able to see over it."

Stanton turned to Jerome. "You wanna go, J?"

"If you want. Sure," the laid-back friend replied.

"I'll get you tickets," Rhyme assured, nodding.

Lilibeth leaned forward and grinned at Rhyme. "Me, too?"

"Absolutely." Rhyme then turned and brushed his lips over Max's temple. "You, too, little" — he cleared his throat — "uh, beloved?"

To Max's surprise, he didn't feel the least bit of offense at Rhyme's near slip. In fact, he sort of missed the endearment.

Max swallowed hard before offering Rhyme a shy smile. "You, um, you can call me that . . . if you want to," he murmured, trying to keep breathing slowly so he didn't blush. "I-I didn't understand before. Didn't listen to . . . how you said it."

"I'd like that very much," Rhyme murmured, cradling his face with his free hand. Tracing his thumb along Max's jaw, he stared into his eyes. "And I *am* sorry that the first words you heard me speak were something that offended you. I didn't mean to. I" — Rhyme paused, grimacing — "I joke and shit, but I never mean to hurt."

Max nodded, hearing the sincerity in Rhyme's tone and reading the truth in his eyes. "Sometimes misunderstandings happen."

"Then going forward," Rhyme began slowly, "we should try to avoid misunderstandings. Hmm?"

The way Rhyme continued to tease the pad of his thumb over Max's skin caused the hairs on his neck to stand on end.

"Y-Yeah," Max responded, struggling to focus on Rhyme's words. "Asking and answering questions would be a good thing."

"Right." Rhyme held his gaze, his voice turning husky. "Communication."

"Yeah. Communication."

"Then we're gonna communicate that we're here," Lilibeth cut in with a giggle. "Just let me slip past you here, and I'll walk with Jerome and Stanton." Lilibeth patted Max's shoulder as she eased by him. "You take your time. I'm sure Rhyme knows the way."

Max nodded absently, but he couldn't seem to take his focus off of Rhyme, and Rhyme stared right back at him. When the jostle of the wagon stilled and the murmur of voices disappeared, Max held his breath.

Will Rhyme really kiss me?

"I had planned to wait until after our date, Max." Rhyme slid his hand up Max's jaw and into his hair. "But you are so damn irresistible." He groaned softly as he lowered his head. "If I kiss you now, will you think less of me?"

"Never," Max breathed against Rhyme's lips, praying he would close the distance. When the big man still hesitated, appearing conflicted, Max ordered, "Kiss me."

With a groan, Rhyme obeyed.

Seconds later, Max felt his head swim as pleasure assaulted his senses in a wave of desire beyond anything he'd ever experienced. He opened his mouth wider, rested his hands on Rhyme's wide chest, and gave himself up to the exquisite sensations.

CHAPTER EIGHT

Bliss. Ecstasy. Delicious rush of flavors.
Rhyme lost himself in the sweet taste of Max's mouth. His beloved tasted better than anything he had ever tasted, could have ever imagined tasting. He swept his tongue deep into Max's mouth again and again, learning the shape of him and reveling in his sweet responses.

Unable to resist, Rhyme nipped a fang over Max's bottom lip. The well of blood almost had him shooting off right that second. Max's iron-rich life-fluid caused his senses to sing and his breath to catch in his throat.

On a groan, Rhyme tore his lips from Max's own. He heard his beloved's whimper and felt his trembles against him. Panting harshly, he rubbed his hands up and down Max's back, attempting to soothe his human even as he struggled to regain control of himself.

"Goddammit, beloved," Rhyme muttered, a rasp in his voice he couldn't help. "Much more of that and I woulda laid you over this hay bale and mounted you, consequences be damned."

And Rhyme knew there would have been consequences. Not only were they way too close to others, but he still needed to explain so much to Max. He needed to explain that vampires and paranormals existed, and that he was one. Plus, Rhyme had to share the fact that Max was his beloved — the other half of his soul.

Gods, bonding with a human is so damn complicated.

"Y-Yeah," Max responded roughly. "That'd probably be

bad." His cheeks were flushed, causing his freckles to stand out in stark relief. "I don't wanna get fired, after all. And you probably wouldn't like that, either."

Rhyme chuckled as he nodded, although he knew that wouldn't happen. His master would be pissed at his carelessness if they were caught. That was mostly due to the number of people's minds the vampires would have to alter.

It was a pain in the butt.

"Come on," Rhyme urged, rising to his feet. He held out his hand, offering it to Max. "Let's go find something to eat."

Max nodded, taking his hand and allowing Rhyme to draw him to his feet. Rhyme began leading him toward the flip-down stairs they used for hayrides. When Max muttered under his breath, Rhyme nearly fell off the wagon.

"If for nothing else, it'll give my dick a second to relax."

Rhyme knew Max hadn't meant for him to hear his whispered grumble, and it took all his self-control to keep from betraying that he'd heard. *Just hot damn.* As Rhyme descended the stairs, he carefully adjusted his erection.

Good thing I decided to wear a nice shirt that could be left untucked.

There was something to be said for planning ahead.

Once Rhyme had reached the bottom, he helped Max descend the staircase, which barely moved under his diminutive human's weight. He didn't mention that, however. His sweet beloved had quite the complex about his size, and Rhyme wondered from where it stemmed.

Something else to figure out . . . eventually.

"This way," Rhyme encouraged, leading Max toward the trees.

A trail appeared between the trunks, the dirt packed hard from the passage of plenty of feet. They heard the chatter of voices and the crackle of a fire long before they saw the gleam of the flames. A moment later, the people appeared in the dim light of the fading sun filtering through the trees.

Rhyme slid his hand down to rub at the small of Max's back. Teasing at his spine through his shirt, he appreciated the tremble that worked through the small sexy body next to him. He spotted several knowing looks on the faces of his beloved's co-workers, and he loved being associated with his human.

Fortunately, the bosses didn't appear to mind at all that Max was using the business outing for a bit of recreational fun. They smiled and greeted them both pleasantly as Rhyme and Max sat down beside Jerome, their scent betraying their amusement. Only Esmerelda scowled at them before turning her attention to the guy sitting next to her, dismissing them.

George chuckled from his position a few places down. "Damn, Max. It sure didn't take you long to change your tune about that cowboy." Waggling his eyebrows, his scent betraying that he teased, he added, "Let me guess. He showed you his big dick, and you couldn't resist." George winked. "Heard you were a queen after all."

Jerome reached over and smacked George upside the head.

"Hey!" George cried, rubbing the back of his head. "What the hell was that for?"

"For being a dumbass," Jerome deadpanned back. Then he turned and addressed the woman sitting next to George. "Sorry, darlin'. If you're gonna date this one, you're gonna have to get used to his unfiltered mouth." Jerome shrugged.

For a second, the blonde glanced between them all . . . and Rhyme scented a hint of unease from George. Then she wrapped one arm around George's own and pressed her sizable tits against him. "Oh, it's all right," she murmured coyly, rubbing her other hand up and down his chest. "I can handle a guy with no filter." She glanced between Jerome and the others while adding, "It's guys that *mean* to hurt with their words that you have to watch out for."

"And their fists," Stanton added, his expression serious.

"Them ain't no good, and you get away from them asap."

"Absolutely right, and excellent advice," Lilibeth stated firmly. Then she patted Rhyme's knee and leveled a serious gaze upon him. "You use your fists to get what you want, Rhyme?"

"No, definitely not," Rhyme immediately replied. Then he smiled and focused on Max. "I'm much more apt to use seduction to get my way."

Lilibeth hummed. "As long as it's not something that will hurt my Max."

Rhyme felt a rush of possessiveness surge through him upon hearing Lilibeth's words.

Max is mine, not hers!

Knowing she didn't mean it the way it sounded, Rhyme ruthlessly shoved it back. Instead, he forced a smile. "Absolutely not. I only want what's best for Max." He realized the conversation should be with his beloved, not his beloved's friend. Turning on the bench seat to focus on Max, Rhyme took his human's hands between his own. "We've just met, so promises are pretty empty since there's so little trust between us. I mean to prove my words when I say that caring for you is my sole focus."

Upon seeing Max's wide-eyed look, Rhyme mentally winced. That had been so close to a declaration of love, and it was way too early for that. As a vampire, however, his feelings developed at super speed, and his words were the truth.

"U-Um, okay." Max's eyes were wide behind his black frames, and he looked a bit shell-shocked. "Th-Thanks?"

Rhyme chuckled softly before dipping his head and pecking a kiss to Max's upturned lips. Then he settled more comfortably on the bench seat, resting his arm along the back so he could cradle Max close. Rhyme glanced around at Max's friends and coworkers, feeling surprisingly relaxed with the group. Well, most of them. Esmerelda was still turning her nose up at them.

Whatever.

"Hey, Laredo," Rhyme called to a fellow vampire who was one of the guys chaperoning the dinner. Due to the fact that Rhyme was an enforcer and Laredo a tracker, the other man immediately paused in his conversation with a guest and gave him his attention. Rhyme smiled at the human who Laredo had been chatting with before asking his friend, "I'm sure inquiring minds would like to know . . . when will dinner be ready?"

Laredo chuckled as he pointed at the array of dinners wrapped in tin foil and cooking in the coals at the edge of the bonfire keeping everyone warm. "Right about now. There's the meat, potatoes, carrots, and onions." Then he pointed over his shoulder toward the covered wagon and the buffet-like rails that ran along the side. "The coleslaw, baked beans, mac and cheese, and apple cobbler will all be waiting there."

Standing, Laredo clapped his hands together. "Welcome again, everyone. How about we start with drinks? There's beer, wine, soft drinks, and juice." Laredo pointed toward several barrels with their lids off. "I've been told it's been verified that everyone on this trip is over twenty-one, so help yourselves."

From his prior outings, Rhyme knew that the barrels of drinks and hot trays of food would be refilled from damn near endless stores kept in the wagon. There was always plenty of everything. Fortunately, everyone in the coven was happy to eat leftovers, too.

Just because there was a dining hall didn't mean everyone ate in it for every meal.

Rhyme stood and shuffled along with the crowd, keeping close to Max's backside. He chose a beer while his beloved picked up a twelve-ounce bottle of merlot. Then they moved into the line for food.

Placing his bottle on his tray, Rhyme skipped the baked

beans in favor of the mac and cheese, coleslaw, and apple cobbler. Max only took mac and cheese and cobbler. Finally, they stood before the fire where Laredo asked what they wanted — hamburger, chicken, or only veggies.

Rhyme and Max both chose the burger meal, and Laredo settled a tin foil package on each of their trays next to their plates of other food. "Enjoy."

"We will. Thanks, Laredo." Rhyme dipped his head in appreciation, and his fellow vampire returned it with a smile. "Come on, handsome."

After they'd settled back on the bench, they both set their trays on their thighs and dug in.

Rhyme took a bite of mac and cheese. As he chewed the soft, melt-in-his-mouth goodness, he carefully unwrapped the hot tin foil. With only a bit of singed skin on his fingertips — which would heal in about fifteen seconds — Rhyme revealed his seasoned hamburger, onions, potato slices, and julienned carrots.

Yum!

Upon seeing Max wave his hand and hearing him hiss, Rhyme hummed. "Here, Max." He carefully picked up and settled his opened container of food onto his beloved's tray, then he grabbed Max's unopened one for himself.

"Wait. Are you sure?"

Rhyme nodded as he began unwrapping the new package with deft moves. "Yeah. No problem, hon." Once he had the second package opened, he winked at Max. "See?"

"Hey, is there ketchup?" someone hollered.

"Blasphemy!" Zane shot back. He was the vampire in charge of stocking the wagon, refilling the trays, and monitoring food. "You take that back right now!" But then he held up a basket and shook it. "Packets of ketchup, mayo, mustard, and even relish for all you crazies." Using a cheeky wink to soften his teasing, Zane walked over and held the basket out to the man who'd spoken.

Everyone laughed for a moment, then began eating. Several others asked for the basket to be passed to them, but it was done in discreet whispers and with plenty of snickering. Even Max took a couple of packets of ketchup and poured them onto his slices of potatoes.

Rhyme snorted as he shook his head when his beloved offered it to him.

Almost two hours later—food eaten and alcohol consumed—Rhyme once again had Max wrapped up in his arms while on the hay wagon. This time, his beloved snuggled against him. While it was probably due to the wine his human had consumed, Rhyme enjoyed it anyway.

Once the ride was over, Rhyme again helped Max from the wagon. He twined their fingers and started them strolling after the others. Biting back a sigh, he tried to think up some way to prolong things.

Unfortunately, Rhyme couldn't think of a single damn thing other than sex or explaining the existence of vampires. He wanted to do both but had reservations. If they had sex, would Max feel like this was a vacation fling? If he explained vampires, would Max think he was nuts and go running?

Gods, this is so hard.

"Is there somewhere we can make out, so I can feel you up?"

Rhyme froze as his gaze snapped to Max. His beloved laughed as he grinned up at him cheekily. Then he shrugged and winked.

"I don't wanna have sex, but I sure would like to get to know you a little better." Max's eyes narrowed behind his glasses as he looked up and down Rhyme's frame in blatant perusal. "And I mean that in the carnal sense of things. We've been good all evening." Max rested his palm on Rhyme's chest and rubbed, fondling his nipples. "Now I want to play a little."

Moaning, Rhyme nodded. "Hell yeah."

Thinking quickly, Rhyme chose a direction and started guiding Max toward a secluded section of the ranch that backed up to the foaling barn—a section out of bounds for guests. It promised a high probability of privacy.

Perfect.

CHAPTER NINE

Max knew it was the alcohol in his system that had him making such a bold statement. As he followed Rhyme into the darkness, he felt damn pleased that he had, however. His body had been primed ever since the hot-as-fuck kiss the big cowboy had laid on him while on the wagon.

I want more of that.

Less than a dozen paces into the trees and Rhyme pulled Max into his arms. He spread his legs as he relaxed against a tree trunk. Max found himself sprawled over the large man's torso. The adjustment of Rhyme's height meant their bodies lined up from groin to shoulders.

Upon feeling Rhyme's erection pressing against his own, Max let out a helpless whimper as he bucked his hips. He searched for friction, but the other man's big hand on his ass didn't allow him to move. Rhyme gripped Max's nape with his other hand, urging him to tip his head up so their gazes clashed.

Seeing the stark need etched across Rhyme's dark features, Max shivered. For just an instant, he thought the other man's eyes flashed with a hint of red. Dismissing that just as quickly as a trick of the moonlight, Max rubbed over Rhyme's wide torso, enjoying the feel of hard flesh under his palms.

"Holy shit," Max whispered, stroking and caressing. "Can I open your shirt?"

Rhyme moaned, and his hands twitched where he held Max. "I so wanted to be a gentleman," he stated, his voice gruff, betraying his need. "You're just so fucking delectable, little bit. Making it so hard."

Max grinned up at Rhyme as he bucked his hips, rubbing his stiff dick against his soon-to-be-lover's equally rigid erection. "I do make you hard," he teased as he worked his fingertips between the edges of Rhyme's pearl-snapped shirt. Without waiting for permission, he tugged. "Can I take advantage of you, Rhyme?"

Then Max popped the first couple of snaps and teased over the warm, firm flesh revealed to him.

Growling, Rhyme dipped his head as he huffed a breath. "Yes, my beloved." The move shielded his face beneath his hat brim, but his words were stark with need. "Do whatever you want with me. I am yours."

Max's heart tripped wildly in his chest.

If only that were true.

Unwilling to pass up an offer like that, Max massaged his left hand under the flap of Rhyme's shirt. At the same time, he began popping the shirt's remaining snaps. He shuddered as he admired the smooth dark flesh revealed to him, all toned and hard muscle.

"Oh wow," Max whispered as he arched his back so he could see more.

The move pressed Max's groin harder against Rhyme's, and his big lover moaned. When Max teased his fingertips down his chest, skimming over his nipples, the cowboy hissed and bucked against him. Only Rhyme's hold on his ass kept Max from tumbling backward.

"Sorry," Rhyme mumbled, massaging Max's nape, offering reassurance. He lifted his head, revealing his lips curved into a harsh, hungry smile of need. "Feel too good. Love your touch. So — "

Feeling emboldened by Rhyme's rasped words, Max cut him off with a twist of his nipple. The big man sucked in a harsh gasp, then let it out on a low groan.

"Max!"

The way Rhyme cried his name, low and guttural and needy, sent Max's heart soaring. That he could reduce such a huge, confident man into a being of such need, sent a burst to his ego the size of a fireball. Max's body thrummed with desire as he spread Rhyme's shirt and teased along his sculpted abdominals.

"Oh, damn, Rhyme," Max whispered, peering up and meeting his gaze. "You're so very stunning."

Rhyme moaned as he shook his head. "Not as stunning as you," he countered, sliding his hand into Max's hair, threading the strands between his fingers. "So beautiful."

Then Max couldn't reply, because Rhyme sealed his mouth over his lips. The big man pushed his tongue into his mouth and plundered it. Max whimpered as the man began to fuck his cavity the way he wished Rhyme would fuck his ass.

Answering Max's noises with a moan of his own, Rhyme teased along his tongue and sucked it into his mouth. When he felt a prick to his tongue, he gasped at the unexpected sting. Then Rhyme teased along his appendage, and the move sent a burst of tingling pleasure through his body.

Issuing a sharp whine, Max tore his mouth from Rhyme's as his body bucked almost spastically. He was on the edge of orgasm . . . and from so little stimulation. His balls tingled and rolled, and his cock throbbed.

"Relax, my beloved," Rhyme crooned into his ear before licking the flesh below there. "I will take care of you."

Rhyme insinuated his hand between their bodies, releasing his neck.

Unable to help himself, Max watched as Rhyme opened first Max's fly, then his own. He used his hold on Max's butt cheek to shift his hips back a little. That allowed him to push down both their briefs.

When Rhyme's long, dark erection burst free of his underwear, Max hummed in approval. Just as he'd noticed in the restroom, the cowboy was long, thick, and uncut. His mouth watered with his desire to tease his lover's foreskin.

"Gods, baby," Rhyme rumbled. "Whatever you're thinking, another time. I promise. I just . . . gods, after all the teasing today." A whine full of need erupted from his throat. "Need release. Need to touch and taste. Please, beloved."

Max yanked his gaze from the beautiful view below and tipped his head back. He took in Rhyme's clenched jaw and flared nostrils. This time, he definitely spotted a hint of red in Rhyme's eyes.

Maybe he has allergies?

In the next instant, Max's thoughts dissolved since Rhyme dipped his head and pressed his lips to his neck. He licked and sucked, teasing along his column of flesh. Tipping his head back, Max offered more room, and Rhyme didn't disappoint. He mouthed sharp, sucking kisses along his flesh.

Max sighed and shivered in his hold. His nipples beaded, and his skin goose bumped. When Rhyme gripped both their shafts in his big hand and began jacking them, Max barked a cry and nearly came out of his skin.

"Come for me," Rhyme crooned, his words slightly garbled seeing as he hadn't lifted his mouth from where he continued to nip, lave, and lick at his neck. "Want to smell you. Taste you. Feel you buck with your pleasure. Spill on me so I can smell you on my skin."

The visual sent Max careening over the edge. His balls pulled tight, his orgasm crashing over him. Opening his mouth on a silent cry, he tipped his head back and rutted spastically.

The sweet bliss created by cresting endorphins sang through his system. Clinging to Rhyme, he shivered against him, delighting in the way the cowboy's calloused hand continued to slowly stroke his sensitive shaft. Just as Max's sensitivity began to become too much, he felt something odd . . . Rhyme's teeth at his neck.

Max gasped as he felt the pop of teeth piercing his skin. Sucking in sharply in surprise, he let that breath out on a moan when his nipples tightened and his balls churned. Then his gut clenched as a second orgasm blindsided him

Sagging against Rhyme, Max bucked in his hold. He vaguely recognized the fact that his lover sucked on his neck as he massaged his ass. Bliss and lethargy pinged through him in equal measure, causing his body to hum pleasantly.

Rhyme lifted his mouth from Max's neck, then licked his tongue across his flesh. The move sent tingles of aftershocks across his skin. He shivered, clinging to the cowboy.

"W-Wow," Max mumbled.

"Mmm-hmm." Rhyme nuzzled his neck for a moment, then lifted his head and smiled languidly at him. "You taste almost as good as you feel." Rubbing his hand up and down Max's spine, he murmured, "So sexy. So responsive. Can't wait to explore you fully."

Tension Max hadn't even been aware of eased from his body, and he rested his whole weight on Rhyme. *This really isn't a vacation hook-up.* He arched his neck so he could stare up and meet his new lover's gaze, ignoring the press of his glasses on his temple. Smiling languidly, he rubbed up and over Rhyme's shoulders, admiring their wide breadth.

Rhyme dipped his head and gave him an awkward kiss. "Okay, little bit. Let's get you back to your bed before you pass out on me."

Max chuckled and nodded. "You wore me out today."

Grinning, Rhyme winked. For just an instant, the moonlight gleamed off Rhyme's teeth, accentuating the sharper than normal canines. Then he murmured, "You've had a lot of activity today," distracting him. He pecked a kiss before offering, "Let's use my shirt to clean up our stomachs before I walk you back to your cabin."

Nodding, Max slowly pushed away from Rhyme. After

making certain his trembling legs would hold him, he took a step backward. Watching Rhyme shrug out of his shirt, he felt a fresh wash of arousal as his dick twitched, and his mouth watered.

Rhyme's nostrils flared as he moaned softly. "Behave, my beloved," he urged softly, holding out his shirt. "I want our next round in a bed."

Nodding slowly, Max took the offered shirt and wiped it over his groin. He didn't know when Rhyme had done it, but the big man had rucked his shirt up, so most of his spend had missed the fabric. Only a bit of the hem had become damp.

Damn thoughtful.

Once Max had cleaned himself off, he handed the fabric back to Rhyme. His lover cleaned himself as Max righted and closed his jeans. After his cowboy had done the same, he tucked his shirt into his back pocket, then held out his hand.

My cowboy. Max smiled as he took Rhyme's hand. *I sure do like the sound of that.*

What would it take to actually keep a man like this?

As they exited the trees and Max again took in the beautiful sprawling ranch where Rhyme worked, doubts assailed him. The gorgeous black man worked at a guest ranch where there were dozens of beautiful people passing through on a weekly basis. How could Max, who lived in the city over forty-five minutes away, compete with that?

Rhyme somehow had a sixth sense for reading Max's mind. "Can I have your phone number?" he asked, squeezing Max's twined fingers. "I want to take you on a date Monday night."

Max snapped his gaze to Rhyme, who winked at him. "I'd say Sunday night, but I figured you'd have things to do after being gone all weekend. Laundry, getting ready for the work-week, and shit."

As much as Max wished otherwise, he had to agree with Rhyme. "Afraid so." They'd reached Max's cabin by then, and he paused at the base of the steps. "So, um . . ." He held out his hand. "Phone?"

Rhyme smiled as he handed over his device. A second later, he heard a muffled chime from the phone in his pocket. After that, Max handed it back.

"There." Max smiled shyly. "Now you have my number."

"Thank you, Max," Rhyme stated, sounding sincere. He cupped Max's jaw and dipped his head. "Dream of me." After whispering those words, he placed a too-chaste, too-short kiss on Max's lips before releasing him and striding into the night.

Then Max turned and headed onto the porch. As quietly as possible, he crept into the dark cabin and, after locking the door, tip-toed to the bedroom. He suddenly felt like a teenager sneaking into the house in the middle of the night.

Rolling his eyes, Max bit back a snicker at his thoughts. He grabbed the same sweatpants and t-shirt he'd used to sleep in the night before and headed to the bathroom. After he'd cleaned up and changed, Max climbed into bed.

Max rested on his back, staring up at the ceiling. His body still hummed with aftershocks, and he smiled in the darkness. He couldn't remember the last time he'd felt so good after only making out and a handjob.

But damn, Rhyme's hands are amazing.

After about five minutes of lying in bed and staring at nothing, Max sighed. He glanced at the clock and realized the problem. The clock read eleven-fifteen at night, and Max didn't normally go to sleep before midnight.

Shit.

Max was just contemplating pulling up the reader app on his cell phone when Stanton rolled over in his bed to his right. Holding his breath, he waited. He hadn't meant to wake his fellow cabin member, after all.

"You still awake, Max?"

Stanton's deep voice sounded softly through the darkness. From his low tone, the big man gave away his uncertainty. He was also not trying to wake Max if he had indeed already fallen asleep.

Not wanting to hurt Stanton's feelings should he somehow figure out that Max had ignored him, he rolled over to face the big man in the other bed. "Sorry. Did I wake you?" he whispered.

"Uh uh. Was waiting up for you."

Okay. Um . . .

"Why?" Realizing how abrupt that was, Max added, "What's up?"

"You never answered me earlier."

Confused, Max tried to figure out what Stanton was talking about. "I-I'm sorry, Stanton. I don't remember." After a second, he urged. "When? Ask me again?"

"Just before Rhyme arrived earlier."

Through the moonlight streaming through the window, Max made out the way Stanton adjusted himself on the bed to cradle his pillow while still focusing on him.

"How come a gay guy wants something so huge up his ass? Wouldn't it hurt?"

Max gaped for a few heartbeats, then snapped his mouth shut. Never in a million years would he have thought Stanton would follow up on that. Then he realized he should have known better.

Stanton didn't have those kinds of hang-ups. That was probably due to living with Jerome, who while straight as an arrow — apparently — was a very open and accepting guy. Jerome had probably talked openly about his brother and homosexuality with him.

Still, a straight guy could only answer so many questions. Did that mean Stanton wasn't so straight? Clearing his throat, Max pushed that thought right out of his mind.

Instead, Max decided to start with the basics. "Do you remember any of your anatomy lessons in high school, Stanton?"

Huffing a sigh, Stanton admitted, "Jerome helped me get a GED. Classes confused me. I'm much better when things are hands on."

Oh. Okay. Wow!

Max really wondered how Stanton and Jerome had met, but he figured it wasn't the time. Instead, he decided to be blunt. That always seemed to work for Jerome.

Still, as delicately as he could, Max explained about the pleasures of a guy's prostate and the sensitivity of some men's inner chute muscles.

To Max's shock, Stanton seemed to absorb it all as if the information was fascinating.

Even after they'd stopped talking, it took a long time for Max to fall asleep.

CHAPTER TEN

R hyme spent lunch with Max on Sunday, but his group left directly after that. Watching his beloved climb into an SUV and disappear down the driveway felt like a stake to the heart. He rubbed at his chest, and when they disappeared from view, heaved a sigh and threw himself into work.

It won't be forever.

That was a promise he made to himself . . . over and over throughout the day.

"How are you holding up?"

Pausing in his task of cleaning out horse stalls, Rhyme peered at Master Jaymes. The big vampire coven master leaned his forearms on the half wall and stared at him with an assessing gaze. His deep brown eyes held a gleam of worry.

Rhyme smiled at his master, appreciating his concern. "I'm fine." Recalling that Jaymes had needed to wait almost two months so his own beloved could come of age before he could claim him, he assured, "It's only been a day, and I have a date with him tomorrow evening."

"That's good." Jaymes nodded as he continued to stare. "Whatever time off you need, you have it. Arrange it with Mathe."

"Thank you, sir." Rhyme had figured as much, but he appreciated hearing the confirmation. "I'll talk to him."

Mathe was the foreman of the ranch even though he was a tracker in the coven. He had a good head for schedules and numbers. It never failed. If the master or second pulled an enforcer or tracker away from the normal rotation without notice due to coven business, Mathe always had two possibilities to fill the gap.

Tapping the wall with his palm, Jaymes nodded. "Keep me posted. Any help you need, you'll get."

"Thanks again."

Resting his forearm on the wall, Jaymes relaxed. "So, tell me about him."

Rhyme placed the rake on the stall wall, then leaned his butt against it. Shoving his hands into his pockets, he tipped his head back and grinned. For the next thirty minutes, he chatted with his master about the human who consumed his thoughts.

"He lives a ways off," Jaymes pointed out as he finally pushed away from the half-wall. "I hope you won't have too much trouble convincing him to move here." Then a gleam of mischief filled his eyes. "Maybe I'll drop by the construction office and put an idea in the boss's mind that he can do a lot of the accounting from here. If he only has to go in a couple of times a week, it may be easier to convince him."

Grinning at his coven master, Rhyme nodded. "Yeah. I'd appreciate that."

Jaymes chuckled as he turned and began heading toward the doorway. "I'll put my head together with Gypsum and come up with a viable excuse to visit there." With a wave, he left the barn, so Rhyme returned to work.

That evening, Rhyme couldn't resist calling his beloved. "Hi, handsome," he rumbled into the phone when he heard Max's greeting.

"Hi, Rhyme," Max responded, sounding shy.

"How's your unpacking coming?" Rhyme asked as he relaxed on his bed in his room. Rhyme closed his eyes and brought up an image of his small, sexy beloved. "Everything coming together for going back to work tomorrow?"

The creak of fabric sounded through the line, telling Rhyme that Max was at least sitting, too. "Yeah. I'm almost through with the laundry. Just waiting for the last load in the dryer," Max told him. "Then I'll hop in the shower and be ready for work."

Groaning softly at the thought of a wet, naked Max, Rhyme muttered, "Gods, I'd love to see that."

"Really?" Max sounded shocked.

Creasing his brows, Rhyme confirmed, "Oh, yeah. I'd soap up my hands and caress your smooth skin. After you were squeaky clean, I'd count each freckle with my tongue." Rhyme's dick thickened beneath the towel he'd wrapped around his waist after his shower. He chuckled huskily as he shoved the fabric aside and gripped his length. "Gods, just thinking about it has me hard as nails."

Max's breath sounded as if it caught in his throat. "Oh my god, you are?"

"Hell yeah." Rhyme began to jack himself slowly, unable to resist giving his aching dick friction. He moaned softly, struggling to concentrate. "I don't know who fucked with your confidence, little bit," he muttered, his voice husky with his arousal. "But you are so damn hot. Your frame is slender and strong. Your hair is brilliant, and I love how it gleams in the sun." His foreskin eased away from his crown with each stroke, and his balls began to tingle, so he spread his legs, giving them more room. "When you swung off your horse yesterday, I practically drooled over your little bubble butt. I wanted to grip it in both hands and squeeze."

Unable to help himself as he thought of his beloved, Rhyme groaned. His stomach clenched as his dick oozed a bead of pre-cum. Swallowing hard, he struggled to keep his breathing even.

It didn't work.

On the next downstroke, Rhyme rasped a moan.

"Oh, god. Are you jacking off?" Max asked, shock filling his voice.

"Oh yeah." Rhyme didn't bother trying to hide it any longer. "I'm lying on my bed thinking about your gorgeous body. All I was wearing was a towel after my shower. I've pushed that aside, and I'm gripping my hard shaft and stroking it." Rhyme grunted as he teased at his frenulum. "Wish it was you playing with my dick, but hearing your voice in my ear sets my blood on fire, Max. Will you talk to me, baby?"

"I-I don't really know what to say," Max murmured.

Rhyme grinned, appreciating how his beloved's voice had taken on a huskiness, too. "Anything, Max," he told him. With a chuckle, he added, "Hell, you could read the ingredients on your shampoo bottle, and I wouldn't care. I just wanna hear your sexy voice."

After a couple of heartbeats, Max offered shyly, "How about I tell you how much I loved sliding my palms over your huge pectorals." His breathing hitched, then he continued, "Your nipples are perfect for sucking and teasing with my tongue. I could nibble them while I trace the lines of your abdominals."

Max cleared his throat as the sound of fabric rustling came through the line.

Rhyme's blood flamed in his veins. A shudder rocked his body as more pre-cum oozed from him. Tingles began working their way up his spine as his cock throbbed.

"Oh yeah," Rhyme responded gruffly. "I would love all of that. Are you getting your dick out, Max?" He growled as he thought about his beloved touching himself while they spoke. "Are you as hard as me?"

"Yes," Max squeaked before he swallowed loud enough to be heard over the phone. "C-Can't believe I'm doing this."

Chuckling gruffly, Rhyme urged, "Wrap your fingers

around your dick, beloved. Pretend it's my hand caressing the sensitive skin of your shaft." Recalling pressing Max's slender erection against his own, Rhyme purred, "Remember how that felt last night? Remember my hand jacking our dicks against each other? How good it felt?"

Max moaned wantonly in his ear, the sound a thing of beauty. "Yes," he said on a pant. "Oh, god, it felt so good. Your rough callouses sliding up and down my shaft." After pausing to let out another groan, Max muttered, "Your cock is so huge. So dark and thick and beautiful. Wanna slide my tongue under your foreskin and push into your slit."

Rhyme huffed a grunt as he teased his fingertips over his crown, pushing aside the foreskin and scraping a nail over his slit. His gut clenched, and his balls tightened. He could practically taste the bliss of release as it teased at his senses.

"W-Would you suck me, Max?" Rhyme groaned at the mental image. "Would you nurse at my crown and tease my balls?"

"Oh god, yes," Max replied, whining and mewling. "I-I want to lick your balls. I'll suck 'em and roll them in my mouth. I—" A long low moan sounded through the line.

Upon hearing the glorious sound, Rhyme stopped fighting his need. He cupped his balls and squeezed, giving his body the final push it needed. His dick jerked in the air where it arched over his abdominals, then began to pulse, spilling his seed in bliss-inducing spurts.

Rhyme growled his pleasure as he released his nuts so that he could take hold of his erection once more. Milking his throbbing flesh, he extended his orgasm. "Oh, Max, gods." Sighing deeply, Rhyme reveled in the delicious sensations of his release. "Gods, that's good, beloved."

Once his shaft stopped twitching in his grip, Rhyme slowed his rhythm and rested his forefingers on his frenulum. He massaged the wrinkled flesh ever-so-gently as he sighed deeply, extending his pleasure. Humming as he enjoyed the aftershocks, Rhyme grinned at the ceiling.

"Gods, Max," Rhyme began when he finally found his tongue. "You're so fucking sexy."

Max groaned through the line. "Don't start up again," he whined. "I'm so tired I'm not sure I can make it to my bed." A second later, he grumbled, "And getting it up again would hurt right now."

Laughing softly, Rhyme murmured, "Oh, beloved. When I get the chance to lay you down on a bed, I will show you how wrong you are." He dreamed of that moment any time he allowed his mind to wander. "Three orgasms? Four?"

"Think pretty highly of yourself, don't you?"

"Well, I did get you off twice with that handjob last night," Rhyme pointed out smugly.

Humming, Max commented, "About that . . . what was up with the biting? Is that a kink of yours?"

Not wanting to have this conversation over the phone, Rhyme racked his sluggish brain for an acceptable response.

"I mean," Max continued absently, "I never realized I liked that before. I think you biting me was what caused that second orgasm. Why would that happen, though?"

Groaning softly, Rhyme opened his eyes and sat up. "This is something I would really prefer to explain face to face," he decided to admit, hoping he could get Max to agree. "It's more than just a kink, and I . . . I, um" —he paused and sighed, running his palm over his bald scalp—"the explanation may surprise you."

Gods. That's the understatement of the century.

"O-Okay." Max sounded as if he was smiling when he added, "Discussions about sexual kinks should definitely be done face to face."

"Thank you, beloved," Rhyme replied, relief coursing through him. Then he glanced around his empty room and flopped back on the bed. "Wish you were here," he admitted with a sigh. "I'd have you curled up in my arms while we make out for half an hour, then we'd start all over again."

Max laughed, the sound making Rhyme smile. "Probably good that I'm not then. I have work tomorrow, after all . . . and I bet you do, too."

"True. But that doesn't stop me from wishing it." Rhyme slid his fingertips through the cum drying on his hairless chest. "Since I can't hold you, I guess I better let you go so we can both clean up."

Sighing, Max murmured, "Yeah. I suppose so."

"I'll see you tomorrow, though." Rhyme could hardly wait. "Can I pick you up at six-thirty?"

"Sounds good, Rhyme."

There was hesitation in Max's voice, so Rhyme waited, hoping he would say more. To his relief, Max did.

"Rhyme, do you pursue guys who come to the ranch often?"

Rhyme realized what Max was really asking.

Why me?

Since Rhyme didn't want to explain about vampires and soul mates over the phone — humans always needed proof — he decided to go with, "Maximus, I realized you were special the second I laid eyes on you. Please believe me, little bit." After a few heartbeats of silence, Rhyme added, "There's something about you that just drew me in, and I knew I needed a chance to get to know you."

After that, Rhyme waited. There wasn't much else he could say until he curled around his beloved and explained vampires.

Fortunately, Max finally stated, "Okay. So, tomorrow?"

"Definitely," Rhyme confirmed. "Go to bed, and dream of me, little bit." He appreciated that Max had given him permission to call him that. The endearment just fit him so well. "I'll definitely dream of you."

Max snickered. "You can't promise that."

"Sure I can. If I don't do it in my sleep, I'll be daydreaming about you."

"You're too much."

Rhyme could practically hear the blush that he just knew was staining Max's cheeks. "Goodnight, Max."

After clearing his throat, Max responded in kind. "Goodnight."

After disconnecting the call, Rhyme pushed to his feet. He left his phone on the nightstand, then went and took a second shower before climbing back into bed.

Just as Rhyme had promised his beloved, he dreamed about him. Of course, that also left him with the issue of waking up hard and wanting. In the early morning light of dawn, Rhyme gripped his dick and daydreamed about Max, too, spilling his fluids all over his chest once more.

Time for another shower.

CHAPTER ELEVEN

Max glanced nervously at Rhyme, where his boyfriend sat behind the wheel.

Boyfriend. God, how did that even happen?

They'd been out on a date every evening that week, and Rhyme had been the epitome of a southern gentleman. He opened doors, pulled out chairs, and even buckled Max's seatbelt for him. He was always on time, and he always ended the date with a goodnight kiss.

Forty-five minutes later, like clockwork, Rhyme would call and tell him that he'd arrived home safely.

As much as Max enjoyed the attention, his dick needed it even more. He was hard as nails just from sitting in the vehicle with Rhyme. On the phone the prior evening, the cowboy had told him to pack an overnight bag, because their date that evening was going to take place at the ranch.

"And I intend to hold you all night long," Rhyme had vowed.

Now Max sat there, hard and aching, as anticipation thrummed through him.

Rhyme groaned as he reached over and gripped Max's thigh. "Oh, beloved." He glanced toward him, then returned his focus to the road. "What are you thinking about so hard over there? I can smell your arousal from here."

"Smell my —" Max snapped his mouth shut as the heat of his blush flooded his cheeks. Except, then he wondered why. After all, Rhyme had been completely upfront about what he intended to do with him that evening. *Speaking of —* "I'm thinking about you fucking me and giving me three or four orgasms tonight."

Max didn't think it was possible, but he would happily succumb to Rhyme's attempts.

Rhyme moaned. Releasing Max's thigh, he pressed the heel of his hand to his groin.

Staring in surprise, Max saw that Rhyme was in the same state as him. He glanced around, taking in the secluded road they were on. Max hummed as he reclined his seat as far as it would go.

Then Max reached for his fly.

"What are you doing?" Rhyme asked, a growl in his voice.

Realizing he hesitated, which was ridiculous since not only had Rhyme seen his dick before, they'd had phone sex every night that week, too, Max unbuttoned. He'd skipped underwear that evening, since he'd hoped to get lucky. As soon as he unzipped, his erection bobbed up from between the flaps.

"Fuck!" Rhyme hissed, and the truck swerved a little before he righted it. "M-Max." His voice sounded deep, thick, and strained. "Are you trying to kill us?"

"Nope," Max quipped back breathlessly as he shoved his jeans down past his knees. "You've been teasing me all week, and this drive is too long." Splaying his legs, Max cradled his balls in one hand and began jacking his dick with his other. "Gotta take the edge off."

"Damn it," Rhyme snarled, and the truck began to slow. "You little tease."

"Not teasing." Max panted softly as heat coiled in his gut. His nipples beaded, and he swiped his thumb over his crown. "You're the tease."

"Not." Rhyme swerved to the side of the road and shoved the truck into park. "Mine."

Then Rhyme turned in his seat and pushed Max's hands away from himself. He rested his weight on the arm of the chair while gripping Max's dick with his left hand. Slowly, too slowly, Rhyme began to jack him.

"*This* is teasing," Rhyme stated gruffly, his eyes alight with a feral intensity.

Shivers racked Max's body as he grabbed the door with his right hand and the side of the seat with his left. He glanced from Rhyme's hungry gaze to his leaking dick and back again.

"Rhyme," he whined, trying to buck his hips to get more friction. "P-Please."

"Oh, handsome," Rhyme growled. "Here's *not* teasing."

Then Rhyme lowered his head and swallowed Max's dick to the root. Hot wet suction surrounded his cock, yanking a howl of pleasure from Max's throat. Rhyme bobbed on his shaft, tracing his length with his tongue, before swiping over his crown. Sinking back onto him, he lodged Max's head in his throat and swallowed.

Unable to help himself, Max moved the hand on the seat to Rhyme's neck. He squeezed as he planted his feet and began bucking. Rhyme pulled off just a smidge, giving him room, and Max took total advantage.

Max fucked Rhyme's face, watching his spit-slicked erection disappear into his lover's mouth over and over. Each time he bumped his cowboy's throat, Rhyme swallowed around the head. Again and again, Max drove into Rhyme's mouth.

When Rhyme hummed, Max felt his balls tighten. His release coiled in his gut. Moaning in dismay, he fought against it, never wanting the exquisite sensations to end.

Rhyme moved a hand between Max's legs and pushed a finger into his ass. With unerring accuracy, he hit Max's prostate. Fire surged through him, burning him from the inside out.

Max screamed as his orgasm burst through him. His body twitched, his cock throbbed, and his seed pulsed from him in bliss-inducing waves. Even spots floated across his vision.

While Rhyme eased up a little on Max's dick, he never stopped sucking. He swallowed everything Max had to give. When his cock grew sensitive and Max whined and shifted in his seat, Rhyme lifted his head, allowing his semi-hard penis to slip from his lips.

Rhyme looked up at him and licked his lips. His eyes glowed with an eerie red light that caused Max's heart rate to spike for a new reason. Gaping, Max watched in shock as Rhyme licked his lips . . . and his fangs.

Holy shit!

"Wh-What are—" Max couldn't convince himself to finish that sentence.

"Easy, my beloved," Rhyme murmured softly. He blinked once, twice, and the red disappeared. Easing his finger from Max's ass, he rubbed over his thigh. "You're completely safe. I would never ever hurt you."

With just those words, Rhyme confirmed what Max hadn't been able to ask. The man was indeed something . . . else. But that couldn't be possible, could it?

As Rhyme helped Max straighten his clothes, all the while keeping his concerned focus on him, Max tried to decide what to think.

"Let's get to the ranch, and I'll explain everything," Rhyme told him softly after Max had zipped and buttoned his pants. Rubbing his thigh, massaging lightly, he added, "Please give me a chance, little bit?"

Maybe it was because Max was still floating on the endorphins of his release, but he nodded. "Okay."

Sighing, his relief practically a palpable thing, Rhyme smiled at him. "Thank you." After a second, he added, "You won't regret it."

Max sure hoped not.

They fell into silence as Rhyme drove.

After a few minutes, for the first time since Max had accepted Rhyme's apology for their misunderstanding, he felt awkward around the man. He sighed and rubbed his hands over his face. The pleasure from his orgasm had faded, and now he felt . . . apprehension.

"It will all be okay, Max," Rhyme stated, glancing his way and giving him a reassuring smile.

It finally hit him. That hadn't been the first time that Rhyme had made a comment like that. It almost seemed as if he could read Max's thoughts.

"Can you read my mind?" Max decided to just throw it out there.

"No, although once we bond, we will be able to share thoughts telepathically."

Max gaped. "T-Telepathically?" That time, he easily finished the sentence. "What are you?"

Rhyme glanced his way, a pained expression on his face. "Are you certain you want to have this conversation in the truck?"

"Yes." *Not really.*

"Okay." Reaching over, Rhyme rested his hand on Max's thigh.

Max couldn't help it. He tensed.

Yanking his hand away, Rhyme sighed.

Max bet the man wouldn't have looked too different if he had smacked him.

"Sorry," Max whispered. "I—" But he didn't know what to say.

Rhyme shook his head. "It's okay. I'll explain." He glanced Max's way again, his hands flexing on the wheel. "First, you need to understand that humans are not alone in the world."

Turning in his seat to focus more fully on Rhyme, Max burst out, "Are you an alien? Are aliens real?"

Chuckling, Rhyme shook his head. "I have no idea if aliens

are real." He tapped his chest, saying, "What I'm saying is that beings which humans would classify as paranormal live and coexists right alongside them." His mouth open, Rhyme hesitated while glancing at him once more. Then he claimed, "I'm a vampire."

Max gaped, jerking back.

"Please calm down, Max," Rhyme pleaded, his voice soft and soothing. "I would never hurt you. You are my beloved. My soul mate. It's why we feel so drawn to each other." While slowing so he could turn into the ranch's long, winding driveway, Rhyme focused on Max. He squeezed Max's thigh gently and stated, "I would lay down my life for yours, Max."

To Max's surprise, feeling Rhyme's warm hand on his leg sent a fissure of warmth spreading through his leg. The sensation traveled up his legs, and his prick actually twitched. He sucked in a harsh gasp as a fresh wave of arousal flooded him.

"H-Holy shit." Max stared at where Rhyme touched him in shock. "How is that possible?"

"That you're becoming aroused again even though I drank your seed just a few minutes ago?" Rhyme looked at his groin, then gave him a lecherous grin. "It's because you are the other half of my soul. We were made for each other."

"I don't believe in that shit," Max countered, shaking his head.

Rhyme shrugged before stopping before the ranch house. After shutting off the engine, he turned and faced Max. "It doesn't matter if you believe in it or not, Max. You still feel the pull." He waved his hand between them. "This thing between you and me, it can't be denied."

Then Rhyme pushed out of the vehicle, closed his door, and rounded the hood.

Too confused to move, Max sat and waited.

When Rhyme opened the door, he picked up Max's backpack first, which had been resting at his feet. Then he reached over Max and unclipped his seatbelt. Finally, Rhyme took a step backward and held out his hand.

"Come on, Max. It's time for me to show you how deep the rabbit hole goes."

Max snorted as he rolled his eyes. "I can't believe you just made a *Matrix* reference." Taking Rhyme's hand, he allowed him to guide him out.

"Actually, I was referring to *Alice in Wonderland*," Rhyme admitted as he closed the door. Resting his hand on Max's lower back, he added, "But I can see where you'd get *The Matrix* out of it, too."

"So, vampires. Are you sure?" Then a thought occurred to Max. "Or is everyone here into role play and this is an act? Because you were out in daylight."

Rhyme laughed, the move showing off his fangs.

It suddenly hit Max . . . the way so many people on the ranch were always so careful about how they smiled. They'd never shown all their teeth. At the time, Max hadn't really thought about it, but if they had fangs, it would make sense.

After Rhyme had sobered, he slung his arm around Max's shoulders and began guiding him through the place. "Whatever you think you know about vampires, forget it. Okay?"

"So . . . you don't drink blood?" Max arched a brow as he peered up at the smiling man. "Because I distinctly remember you biting me."

Rhyme rolled his eyes. "Okay. Yes, that one thing is true, but everything else is wrong." He lightly squeezed Max's waist, then slid his hand down to cup his butt. "We aren't allergic to sun, garlic, or holy water. We can't turn someone else into a vampire." Then Rhyme winked as he quipped, "Like the song says, we're born this way, baby."

Max snickered as he peered around wide-eyed at all the

gorgeous wood floors, river rock fireplace, and high end, sturdy-looking furniture.

"I'll give you a real tour later, but if you ever get lost, return to here." Rhyme pointed at the room which appeared to be a living room or lounge. "Then I'll know where to find you."

Nodding, Max silently agreed. "Okay. So what's this beloved soul mate business?"

As Rhyme hummed, he led Max back out of the room and toward a set of stairs. "Well, vampires live a long time. Upward of five hundred years," he told him, staring intently at him, as if trying to do the mind-reading thing he seemed to be able to do . . . even though he denied it. "So to alleviate the loneliness such a long life could cause, Fate gives us a beloved. A soul mate. Someone who, once we find them, will complement us and be our one and only throughout those long years." Reaching the top of the stairs, Rhyme paused and pulled him into his arms. "Once we bond, we will do anything for that person. Lay down our life for them. Dote on them. Their happiness and safety is our primary concern . . . in all things."

Max's mind reeled. That had been a lot to take in. It wasn't until a door closed that Max realized Rhyme had started them moving again. Then he was turned and guided to a sofa.

"Please talk to me, Max," Rhyme encouraged.

Cocking his head, Max tried to think of something to say. He recalled the last week . . . how Rhyme had done exactly as he'd told him. Rhyme had cared for him, pleasured him, and damn near swept Max off his feet.

Lilibeth had given him so much crap every day because Max had been on cloud nine all week.

And I want that to continue.

That conclusion led to only one question. Threading his fingers with Rhyme's, he took in his lover's worried expression. Squeezing the vampire's hands — *holy shit, vampires are real* — Max asked, "How do we bond?"

CHAPTER TWELVE

R hyme's jaw sagged open as shock hit him.
Did Max really just ask that?

Staring at his redheaded lover, who was smiling mischievously at him, Rhyme realized that yes, he had. He growled softly as renewed arousal surged through him. His cock had softened when Max had begun to panic, which had actually been a relief.

Sitting in the truck smelling Max's arousal, then drinking his seed, had nearly had him shooting off in his jeans.

With Max sitting on Rhyme's sofa asking about bonding, his dick thickened right back up.

"Sex," Rhyme finally managed to get out of his suddenly too-dry throat. "Sex and blood." Clearing his throat, he added, "I would need to spill in you and drink your blood."

Max rubbed his palms over his thighs. "I-I've never had unprotected sex before." Cocking his head, he nibbled his bottom lip. "W-We'd have to be committed. Ya know? Um, monogamous, and get tested. I—"

Rhyme squeezed Max's fingers. "There are a couple more things. Paranormals cannot get or pass on human diseases." Looks like he'd forgotten something rather important. Upon seeing Max's questioning expression, Rhyme told him, "You're it for me, Max. I will never stray." Then he rolled his eyes. "Hell, after I bond with you, I won't even be able to get it up for anyone else." Then another thought struck, and he growled. "And if anyone else ever touches you, I will fucking destroy them."

Max's eyes widened. "Oh! I—" His brows furrowed, the scent of shock rolling over him. "Really?"

"Yes, really." Lifting Max's fingers to his lips, Rhyme admitted, "Paranormals do things fast. After I bond with you, I will want you to live here with me." Upon seeing Max's jaw sag open, he quickly added, "I know it's a long commute, so maybe we can convince your bosses that you can do your work from home several days a week."

Groaning, Rhyme added, "Shit, there's so much to explain." He rubbed his palm over his scalp while saying, "You asked earlier if I could read your mind. I told you the truth when I said I couldn't. It can seem that way because we do have a better sense of smell, and when you're upset or aroused, I can smell it." Upon seeing Max's eyes widen and his cheeks pink, Rhyme hurried to add, "A vampire also has the ability to alter memories, so people don't remember us feeding from them, but I can't with you, because you're my beloved."

Max slowly breathed, his eyebrows furrowing. For a long moment, he stared at where Rhyme still held his hand. His jaw clenched, and so many expressions flitted across his face.

Finally, Max met his gaze. "So, I'm yours, and you're mine." When Rhyme nodded, he asked, "But I only live for several decades. What happens when I die?"

"Oh. Another thing." Rhyme scoffed. "Sorry. There's a lot."

Max just nodded.

"When we bond, your life extends to match mine, so we'll have a long time to live together." Rhyme figured telling Max he was only one hundred thirty-eight years old and that they would have upward of three hundred and fifty years together could wait until another time.

"It's a lot to take in, Rhyme," Max finally whispered, lifting his chin and meeting his gaze.

For one heart-stopping moment, Rhyme thought Max would deny him . . . or ask for more time.

Then Max smiled, his green eyes twinkling behind his black-rimmed glasses. "Are you gonna show me your bedroom before or after dinner?"

Moaning, Rhyme jumped to his feet. He grabbed Max's hips, then lifted him and tossed him over his shoulder. His beloved grunted before erupting into laughter as Rhyme rushed to his bedroom.

"Oh, beloved," Rhyme said on a moan as he carefully laid him out on his comforter. "Don't move."

Then Rhyme whipped his shirt over his head as he kicked off his boots. He shucked his pants, taking his socks with them. Straightening, he burst with pride upon seeing the appreciative gleam in Max's deep eyes.

"I would have helped you with that," Max stated huskily.

"Next time," Rhyme offered, gripping his dick and giving it a cursory stroke. He ached for friction, his balls tingling pleasantly, but he wanted his beloved even more. Drawing on wells of self-control he didn't realize he had, Rhyme released himself. "Now to take care of you."

Rhyme gripped Max's sneaker and pulled it off, followed by his sock.

Max chuckled as his toes twitched, betraying his ticklishness. "I think you already took care of me." He pointed at Rhyme's swinging dick. "It's you who needs to be taken care of." Then Max licked his lips obscenely.

Moaning, Rhyme felt his cock twitch. "Yes, please." He wasn't above begging, but first — "After I undress you."

As much as Rhyme wanted to take his time, he'd been good all week. His nerves were shot, and his need beat at his self-control like waves against a rocky surf. He needed his beloved so damn bad.

"Yeah. Hurry," Max urged, lifting his hips for Rhyme to

pull off his jeans.

Rhyme then gripped the hem of Max's polo and tugged it over his head. When he pulled the fabric free of his lover, his beloved's glasses were askew, and his hair was wild. His gaze was heavy-lidded, and his eyes were dark with desire.

"So fucking gorgeous," Rhyme rumbled as he climbed onto the bed. Settling on the bed beside Max, he rested his weight on his right elbow. "Love these," he commented as he slowly traced along Max's slender shoulder and the freckles covering them. "So many. Can't wait to count them."

"You're the gorgeous one," Max countered, rubbing his palms over Rhyme's pectorals. Then he skimmed his fingers up to his shoulders and massaged over them. "It's like you have boulders for shoulders and" – Max scraped his nails down again and tweaked Rhyme's nipples – "these nubs are begging to be sucked."

Moaning, Rhyme stared at Max as hunger surged through him. His cock throbbed where it jutted from his groin, leaking with need. His balls felt heavy and swollen, full to bursting with seed he wanted to use to mark his beloved.

"Oh, but this looks like it needs to be appreciated even more," Max all but purred, lowing his hand and cupping Rhyme's aching erection.

Rhyme barked a harsh cry as he bucked into Max's hold, his body moving beyond his control. "M-Max." He would forever deny the whine in his voice as he rutted into the tight grip his beloved had on him.

"Come up here, Rhyme," Max demanded, squeezing his member. "I wanna taste you."

"Yes!"

Rhyme moved swiftly. Reaching under his pillow, he grabbed the lube he'd left there after jacking off that morning. Then he straddled Max's head with his knees while placing his elbow next to his beloved's hip.

As Rhyme popped open the lube, he felt the first wet slide of Max's tongue sliding up his stalk. "Oh, fuck," he whined before pouring a liberal dollop onto his fingers. Burying his nose in Max's red pubes, he inhaled deeply. His senses filled with his human's earthy, masculine aroma, and Rhyme moaned again. Then he wrapped his lips around his beloved's crown and sucked lightly. At the same time, he pressed his slick-dampened fingers to Max's hole.

Max moaned around Rhyme's dick, sending shocks of exquisite sensation through his length. While Rhyme knew that it wouldn't be long before he lost control of his aching testicles, he wanted his beloved to come with him. He utilized his many years of experience and began working Max open in earnest, mercilessly teasing his prostate.

By the time Rhyme had three fingers in Max's chute, his little lover was moaning around his dick. His human's cock leaked copiously into his mouth, offering him a teasing taste of the goodness Rhyme knew he would soon spill. When he pushed in a fourth finger, he rubbed at Max's prostate while rolling his balls and sucking hard.

With a choking scream, Max came. Stream after stream of his beloved's sweet cream filled his mouth. He gulped it down, relishing the slightly salty flavor.

As soon as Max's orgasm began to wind down, his beloved squeezed Rhyme's balls. Groaning around his mouthful, he stopped trying to fight it. His release crashed through him, sending his senses soaring in ecstasy.

Panting harshly, Rhyme allowed Max's half-hard prick to slide from between his lips. He rested his sweaty cheek against his beloved's thigh as he moaned. Only his fear of hurting Max with his big dick kept his hips from rocking.

All the while, Rhyme remembered to keep his fingers embedded in his man.

While Rhyme stopped spurting, his dick continued to

twitch. He nuzzled his nose against Max's ball sack, relishing the intimate scent of his man. Sighing, he barely managed to keep from collapsing on his much smaller lover.

Rhyme stayed that way for several long moments. Then he felt Max slide his tongue under his foreskin, causing tingles to erupt through his groin. When his man shifted his head and suckled ever-so-lightly on his foreskin, Rhyme belted out a cry of delight.

His cock throbbing once more, Rhyme pulled away from Max. He gently eased his fingers from his lover's channel before spinning around. Settling between Max's spread legs, he stared down at his beloved, taking in his flushed body and swollen lips.

"Oh, little bit," Rhyme crooned as he levered over him.

Threading his clean fingers through Max's hair, Rhyme gripped his length with his other hand. As he jacked himself, slicking his shaft, he pressed a kiss to Max's lips, then licked inside. Upon tasting himself on his human's tongue, Rhyme groaned and touched his tongue to the other man's. When breathing became necessary, Rhyme broke the kiss, smiling upon seeing Max's glazed expression.

While scratching Max's scalp lightly, Rhyme asked, "Would you like me to take you like this? Or would you prefer to ride me?"

Rhyme knew he was a big man, and if Max was on top, he would have more control over how much he took of him and how fast.

Max glanced down at Rhyme's length, then met his gaze. "You wouldn't mind if we did that?"

"I would love to watch you bounce on my cock, beloved," Rhyme crooned hungrily.

After another second, Max nodded. "Yes, please."

Rhyme lifted up, then flopped to the right and rolled to his back. Reaching out, he helped Max straddle his hips. Then he gripped his slicked erection in one hand and his beloved's hip with the other.

"Take your time," Rhyme urged, even though all he wanted to do was buck up and sink deep into his beloved's ass.

Max nodded, then began his descent. As soon as his sweet human's anus touched Rhyme's crown, Max inhaled deeply, then let it out on a long breath. For a few heartbeats, nothing happened, then Max's muscled ring stretched, and Rhyme's knob sank inside his lover's body.

Groaning at the exquisite squeeze to his cock's head, Rhyme sucked in a harsh breath. He tensed his muscles, barely refraining from thrusting. Panting harshly, he watched as Max did the same.

The slight wince of pain helped Rhyme keep in control, too.

"W-Wow," Max mumbled. "You're huge."

Rhyme nodded, knowing his cock was bigger and longer than average. While beads of sweat dripped down his temples, he felt relief that he'd offered this position. Never did he want to hurt his beloved.

After what felt like hours, but Rhyme knew was only a minute or two, Max began lowering himself. His beloved took his time, lifting and lowering, and Rhyme gripped the comforter in an attempt to keep himself still. He watched with agonizing anticipation as Max's sweet little hole stretched and swallowed his cock.

"Oh, wow," Max mumbled, finally resting his ass against Rhyme's groin. He panted between parted lips for a few seconds before meeting Rhyme's gaze. While blushing, Max admitted, "I wasn't certain I could take you."

Rhyme rubbed Max's thighs. "I knew you could do it." Moving his hand to his beloved's groin, he began to jack Max's dick. It had softened a little while Max had sank onto him, so he brought it back to full arousal. "You were made for me," Rhyme countered, cradling and rolling Max's ball sack. "You are perfect, my beloved."

Max's chin tipped up, and he groaned. After a few seconds, he began to move. Ever-so-slowly, he rose up a bit, rutting into Rhyme's fingers, then sank back onto his thickness.

Gasping, Max rested his palms on Rhyme's torso. As his movements became sure, he opened his mouth and began to pant. His pulse thudded under his flesh, making Rhyme's mouth water and his fangs ache.

"You gonna come for me, my beloved?" Rhyme desperately wanted that, wanted to be painted with his beloved's seed. "Spray me, Max," he urged. "Mark me. I'm yours."

Max shuddered as he held Rhyme's gaze. With his jaw slack, he slammed down onto Rhyme's erection once more, then froze. His dick throbbed in his hold, pulsing and spewing streak after streak of seed across Rhyme's torso.

The gorgeous view of Max painting his torso caused his balls to tingle. Combined with the breath-taking squeeze to his erection, Rhyme lost any hope for control. His testicles tightened, and his cock shot, erupting within the confines of his beloved's channel.

Wrapping his arms around Max's torso, Rhyme encouraged him down. As soon as his neck came within striking distance, he sank his fangs deep into his flesh. His beloved's delicious life-fluid burst across his taste buds.

Rhyme moaned against Max's sweet skin. He licked and sucked, filling his mouth over and over with his human's blood and twining their lives for eternity. Feeling his lover tremble in his grip as well as the warmth of more seed spreading between them, Rhyme gloried in the knowledge that he'd pleased Max once again.

Easing his teeth from Max's shoulder, Rhyme swiped over the bite wound, closing it. He hummed as he licked his lips, enjoying the sight of the small, beautiful scar he'd left behind.

My mark.

"My beloved," Rhyme whispered into Max's ear. Holding him close, he rubbed up and down his spine as he nuzzled his temple. "So perfect. So beautiful. And all mine."

Max turned his head and smiled up at him. "Okay. I'll move in."

"You will?" Rhyme grinned, even as shock filled him.

"Mmm-hmm." Then Max's eyes took on a mischievous gleam. "As long as you promise multiple orgasms every night."

Barking a laugh, Rhyme planted a hard peck to his mouth before whispering, "Done."

YOU MAY ALSO ENJOY THE FOLLOWING FROM EXTASY BOOKS INC:

A Vampire For His Own
Charlie Richards
Release date

Excerpt

Three days later, Basques drove a coven SUV deep into the woods. Second Ridger sat in the passenger seat, staring out the windshield. Enforcer Carmine and Tracker Kraymer sat in the middle captains chairs.

As they turned to head down a long, winding driveway, Kraymer leaned forward and asked, "Have you guys ever met a gargoyle before?"

Basques glanced in his rearview mirror at the excited expression on the young tracker's face. At barely thirty-eight, the vampire was still considered wet behind the ears, regardless of his extraordinary aptitude for tracking. Times like these reminded Basques of that fact.

"Yeah," Ridger answered. "We visited this clutch almost fifty years ago and met with Chieftain Grecian." Smirking, he added, "He was sort of a dick."

"Hopefully Chieftain Kinsey will be an improvement,"

Basques commented. Then he admitted, "But if he was brutish enough to fight through the inner circle and still beat Grecian, well . . . I'm not holding out much hope."

"Remember to be on your best behavior," Ridger warned. "We would prefer to keep the peace."

"Why would they want a fight, anyway?" Kraymer asked, his confusion clear in his tone. "What use would living near a city be to gargoyles in hiding?"

"Maybe to help them find mates easier?" Carmine guessed before shrugging his wide shoulders. "Doesn't matter. That's our home, and they can't have it." He grinned, showing off his fangs. "But I'll be good."

Ridger snorted. "Glad to hear it."

"Especially since we're here," Basques commented with a chuckle, parking the vehicle to the left of the large lodge-style home's big, four-car garage. "You two pull the mead barrels out of the back while we knock."

"Yes, sir," both men replied almost in unison.

As soon as Basques slipped from the vehicle, the hairs on his nape once again stood on end. He ignored the desire to rub them, unwilling to betray his unease. As paranormals, the gargoyles would be able to scent it easily enough as it was.

"Looks like the welcoming party," Ridger murmured as soon as Basques joined him beside the passenger door.

Basques followed his second's gaze to the front door, which stood open. Three gargoyles were standing on the deck. All three stood well over six feet tall, probably pushing six-foot-six and up. As was traditional for a gargoyle, they all wore a loincloth around their hips, which showcased their thickly muscled torsos and limbs.

The biggest of the lot at around six-foot-ten, a dark-green gargoyle, spoke as Basques and Ridger approached.

"Welcome to the Aerasceatle clutch," he greeted, holding out his black-clawed hand. "I'm Second Destrawn."

"Second Ridger," the vampire greeted, taking the male's

hand. "And this is Head Enforcer Basques. Thank you for allowing us in your people's territory today."

Destrawn offered a wide, toothy smile. "You come bearing aged mead, so of course, we'd say yes." He took a step backward as he chuckled. "That and we know your coven was on cordial terms with this clutch's prior chieftain. It's only natural that you'd want to meet the new one." Beckoning, Destrawn added, "Come on. I'll introduce you to Chieftain Kinsey."

Basques flanked Ridger, falling into step at his left shoulder. He noticed that Carmine and Kraymer handed off the mead barrels to the other pair of gargoyles who'd been waiting on the porch. Then the vampire pair flanked Basques and Ridger.

Destrawn led the way down the hall and through a door on the right, not caring in the least when the pair with the mead went another direction. Basques figured the massive, six-foot-ten gargoyle was either confident in his skills or figured they weren't a threat. When they entered the room, Basques decided it was a little bit of both.

Three others waited.

A big, broad gargoyle with yellowish-orange skin stood on the far side of the large great room near the fireplace. He was the shortest at around six-foot-six and had his arm around a small, slender human. A powder-gray gargoyle stood near a sofa, and he split the difference at six-foot-eight.

Gods, I forgot how big these fuckers can be.

As Basques had suspected, the male holding the human introduced himself as Chieftain Kinsey. The human was his mate, Jimmy. Basques learned that the gray male was Enforcer Sethnos.

They had just finished introductions and pleasantries when a soft knock sounded on the door. Second Destrawn crossed to the door and opened it, revealing a gargoyle smaller than Basques had ever seen before. He was pushing a trolley which held an array of drinks and finger foods.

The pale-blue-hided gargoyle only stood five-foot-ten, and his long white hair hung almost to his waist, even in the half dozen braids it was kept in. Not only that, but the male didn't appear to have any wings, although Basques did spot some extra folds of skin along his underarms and sides.

Huh. Odd.

Just as Basques turned his attention back to Chieftain Kinsey, who was offering them refreshments, a rich, earthy scent tickled his senses. Inhaling deeply, Basques almost groaned. The mouth-watering fragrance seemed to combine with blood-rich iron in a way that slammed him with lust.

For the first time in centuries, Basques's control slipped. His eyes hazed as he riveted his gaze back on the little gargoyle. Groaning, he mapped the heated lines flowing through the small male.

Realization hit.

Holy shit! I think this male is my beloved.

In hindsight, Basques realized he should have said that out loud, but instead, he blurted, "Gods, I want your blood in the worst way."

ABOUT THE AUTHOR

Charlie started writing fantasy when she was eight, and after stumbling onto her first erotic romance at age nineteen, she realized her true calling. She now focuses on writing gay erotic romance, normally of the paranormal variety, with heroes of all kinds. With the help and support of her husband, Charlie finally fulfilled one of her life-long goals . . . move to acreage with her horses. You can often find her curled up with her laptop and a cup of tea or glass of wine, creating her next adventure. Charlie enjoys exploring the mountains of her new Oregon home on horseback, 4-wheeler, or motorcycle.

She can be reached at ch.richards2010@yahoo.com
Or visit her at www.charlie-richards.com